MASSACRE MOUNTAIN

MASSACRE MOUNTAIN

•

C. Jack Lewis

AVALON BOOKS
NEW YORK

PRINTED IN THE UNITED STATES OF AMERICA
ON ACID-FREE PAPER
BY HADDON CRAFTSMEN, BLOOMSBURG, PENNSYLVANIA

This one is for Calvin,
who rides tall in the saddle!

Chapter One

Steve Bard drew his horse to a halt as he topped the last rise and paused to look over the valley below him. It was perhaps two miles wide and the mountains flanking it were steep. Pinion trees thick on the slopes clung to the steepness, while a few ponderosa pines towered above them. The valley between the flanking peaks was a virtual desert, a few stunted junipers growing in clumps. There was knee-high grass, but it was brown for lack of rain and was slowly turning to the same dust that had nurtured it in a less dry period.

It had been a long climb and Bard sat his saddle quietly, allowing the big gelding to draw in long draughts of the clear dry air, while he spent several minutes surveying the area ahead. He had come south from Denver on the Denver and Rio Grande rail line to Santa Fe, where he had unloaded his horse from the stock car. After packing his saddle-bags with a few provisions, he had headed west out of the historic city four days ago. The maps he had been able to obtain of the area were railroad survey maps and didn't offer a great deal of information beyond the route of the tracks.

He had crossed the Rio Grande on a ferry the first day west

1

of Santa Fe and on the second afternoon had been forced to swim his horse across a lesser stream he took to be the Rio Puerco. There were plenty of trails, he had noted, running north and south, but a man was pretty much on his own when it came to traveling west. On the third day, he had crossed the Cabelleta Mountains and in the haze ahead had spotted the extended range that had to be the Continental Divide. It had taken him the fourth day to reach the divide and find the landmark known as Powell Mountain. The pass that led across the divide peaked at some 8,500 feet before it started down.

From the top of the pass where he sat his horse, Bard could see numerous canyons that branched off from the valley below, most appearing as crude slashes in the rock faces of the mountains. Boulders at the edge of the valley no doubt had tumbled down from the mountains in centuries past. The trail he had taken over the pass had been dim and little used. It no doubt was used more by Indian hunting parties than anyone else, but he could see that it ran through the valley's grasslands in the general direction of Fort Wingate, where he was headed.

Steve Bard was dressed in dark blue cavalry trousers of which the yellow stripe had been removed from the outer seam on each leg. He wore cavalry boots without spurs, while his upper body was covered by a grimy buckskin jacket that had seen a lot of hard wear. If one looked closely, there were two holes in the rough-out leather that could have been made by bullets. There was no sign of blood, so it could be supposed the holes resulted from bullets that killed the deer from which the buckskin was made.

The hat Bard wore was fairly new and was the flat-crowned type seen in the Southwest, where there wasn't much rain. Belted over the buckskin jacket was a wide pistol belt with ammunition filling most of the sewn loops. A holster on his left hip carried a Colt Single Action Army revolver, which had been introduced only a year earlier in 1873. Most of the guns had been supplied to the United States army, but Colt was also selling a few to civilians at $26 each. The price was considered high, suggesting the reason so few were being sold outside of military channels. In the saddle scabbard hanging from his saddle was a Winchester 1873 carbine with a twenty-inch barrel. It fired the same cartridge as the revolver, the .44.40 caliber loaded with black powder.

In his flat-heeled boots, Bard stood a couple of inches over six feet. The buckskin jacket tended to make him appear heavier than his 180 pounds that were composed primarily of bone and muscle. The man's hair was brown below his hat, hanging below the collar of the jacket. The sun had bleached some of it until the strands formed an unusual pattern. He had high cheekbones that suggested he might carry some Indian blood, but his eyes were a deep-lake blue, the same shade seen in the eyes of such notorious gunmen as Jesse James and Wild Bill Hickok. His face wore the four days of beard grown since he had left Santa Fe, but where skin was visible, it was a deep shade of sun-tanned brown. There was a slight hump in his nose that indicated it had been broken at least once and not reset to its original straightness.

Bard allowed perhaps five minutes for the horse to regain its strength. By that time, the flanks no longer were quivering and the animal's breathing had returned to near normal. Along the animal's shoulders some of the sweat was even beginning to dry with a cresting of salt on the stiff, matted hair. Bard folded the map he had been checking and returned it to one of his saddlebags before he touched the horse's belly with his boot heel and lifted the reins in signal. The horse began its downward trek into the valley.

Bard had ridden no more than half a mile, when there was

the sound of a shot and a bullet kicked up dust less than a yard ahead of his horse. Then came a cry that verged on a scream. He turned his head to see five horsemen coming out of one of the canyons to his rear, their horses at a dead run. *Indians!*

Bard realized his own horse was too spent to outrun the Indian ponies, but he heeled the horse into a run that would eat up ground. That was when he spotted another half dozen Indians charging directly toward him. Most of them, he saw, carried rifles. He pulled his mount to a sliding halt, glancing to the rear to see how close the first band was. They were coming fast. Almost as though he had rehearsed the move, the rider reined the horse toward the left side of the valley, heading directly toward one of the canyons, urging the big gelding to a run once more.

At the mouth of the canyon, Bard pulled up, digging in the pocket of his jacket for a block of sulphur matches. He tore one off, struck it and dropped it into the brown grass at his horse's feet. For a moment, he thought the match had gone out, then there was a flame. Five seconds later, the fire was spreading, eating the dry prairie grass that was almost two feet high. There were more shots and Bard ducked as he heard a ricochet scream off the canyon's rock face a few yards away.

With the prairie fire blazing and the draft from the canyon driving the flames and covering smoke toward the Indians, Bard urged his horse farther into the wide cleft between the canyon walls. After a few yards, they came to a downed pinion tree that appeared to have been uprooted to tumble down the mountain. It almost blocked the canyon, but Bard was able to edge his horse around the extended dead branches.

On the other side, he dismounted and dropped the reins to ground-tie the gelding. He moved to the pinion and dug a folding knife from his pocket to scrape some of the bark from the trunk of the downed tree. It fell in a heap just under

the trunk. Satisfied with the amount of tinder he had created, Bard struck another of the sulphur matches and held it to
the crumbled bark. He knew from experience that Indians
often carried packets of pinion bark with them to help in
building fires.

The bark caught fire immediately and in less than two
minutes some of the dead foliage of the tree had also caught
fire. The horse didn't like being so close to the blaze and
glanced back to see what was happening.

"When they get through that burned grass, this oughta
keep them back for a time," Bard told the horse as though the
animal deserved an explanation. He rose and backed away
as other parts of the tree began to burn, forming a wall of
blocking fire.

Slipping the matches back into his pocket, Bard mounted
the horse and began to negotiate the rough floor of the canyon,
reining the horse around sharp rocks that extended above the
sand that had been washed through the narrow gorge over the
thousands of years.

Bard was puzzled by the bands of Indians that had jumped
him. They wore no feathers in their hair. As near as he could
see, none of them had painted faces indicating they were
seeking trouble. It might have been a hunting party, but if so,
why would they attack him? This was the land of the Navajo,
a tribe that was supposedly at peace with the white man.

Bard, a Texan by birth, had fought as a Confederate cavalry officer in the War Between the States. Captured, he had
been imprisoned with other southern soldiers until he had been
given the opportunity, with a few others, to be paroled from
the Yankee's hated Andersonville Prison and shipped west to
fight Indians on behalf of the Union.

Following the conditions of his parole, Bard had served
with cavalry units that had fought Comanches along the
frontier until the war had ended. Instead of going back to

Corpus Christi, his original home, he had signed on with the United States Cavalry as a civilian scout. That had been eight years ago and most of those years had been spent in scouting against Comanches, the Lakota Sioux and the Arapahoes.

He had been a contract employee and when his time was up, he had gone to Denver for what he considered a long-overdue vacation. As he rode through the canyon, he considered those past few weeks. He had gambled with the wrong people and in a fit of conscience or perhaps guilt had given $200 to a saloon girl, who told him she wanted to leave her tawdry, pointless life and go home to Alabama.

He'd seen the woman a night or two later, trying the same scam on a silver miner who had struck it rich. By then nearly broke, Bard's first inclination had been to expose her to the miner, then try to shake his own money out of her. A glance about the saloon, though, convinced him that she undoubtedly had more friends there than he. Broke and disgusted, he had found the local cavalry headquarters and signed on once again as a contract scout. The officer who signed his papers assured him his new assignment would be totally unlike what he had been through with the northern tribes. He was to report to Fort Wingate in New Mexico Territory.

"The Indians are all on reservations," the cavalry recruiter had assured him. "It should be a pretty easy tour of duty."

Bard uttered an ironic chuckle as he rode up the canyon, recalling that conversation. It occurred to him he just might be on a Navajo reservation at this time, but that was no reason for them to be chasing him. Navajos or not, it was still government land.

As the walls of the canyon began to pinch closer together, Steve Bard had a new problem to consider. He didn't know what lay ahead in the twisting canyon. He might well run into a blank wall up ahead. Solid rock in front of him maybe, Indians behind him for sure. And that dead pinion tree wasn't going to burn forever!

Chapter Two

Half a mile or so up the canyon, Bard came upon another obstacle, a ponderosa pine that had fallen into the cleft, nearly blocking the passage. The downfall was old and rotten. Beneath it, its pine needles had disintegrated to tinder. By breaking off a few dead limbs, he was able to get his horse over the trunk of the downed tree. Looking back the way he had come, he saw smoke rising above the rim of the canyon. Another fire wouldn't hurt. If they got this far, maybe the Indians would figure chasing him was more trouble than his scalp was worth!

Again, using sulfur matches from the block he carried, he lit the broken pine needles beneath the tree trunk. It was only minutes before the rotting tree was fully ablaze. Since it was larger than the pinion he had fired earlier, the flames were higher and the smoke considerably thicker.

Back in the saddle, he rode on, still worrying about what he would find at the end of the cleft. Was he in a box canyon or was there a way out at the other end?

The answer came soon enough. At first glance, it appeared the canyon ended with what appeared to be a sheer wall of solid granite. A man might be able to climb it without falling, but that would leave him afoot at the top. As he rode close to the left wall of the canyon, closer inspection showed indications of what might have been a vague, rock-strewn trail that seemed to angle upward.

Dismounting to inspect the ground, Bard found tracks that he judged to be those of elk. He glanced at his horse, pondering for a moment before he picked up the reins and started up the trail afoot, leading the reluctant horse. If an elk could make it, the horse should be able to follow him, he reasoned.

In spots, portions of the narrow ledge had broken off, the trail being nearly obliterated. It took great patience to urge the big dun gelding across these spaces. Halfway up, eighty feet or so above the canyon floor, the horse's weight caused the ledge to crumble and it fell away beneath the animal's hind feet. Screaming its fear, the panicked horse scrambled forward seeking to save itself. The animal's shoulder caught Bard and almost sent him plummeting off the trail and into the canyon below. Both feet were over the edge of the trail when he grabbed the horse's breast collar and allowed the fearful horse to drag him back to the narrow ledge. Suddenly feeling safe, the horse halted, its whole body shaking. Bard's buckskin jacket was dark with perspiration born of fear, the horse's profuse sweating caused by the same emotion.

The trail became somewhat easier as they neared the top of the canyon wall and Bard held up, allowing himself and the horse to breathe in a feeling of relief. Looking back down the canyon, the burning ponderosa pine was invisible around a bend, but dark smoke was rising into the sky from its hidden location.

There were no cries from the Indians and Bard hoped they had given up. It did occur to him that they would know the country and might be waiting ahead for him to come out of the canyon. That thought brought on a new wave of caution, as he began to lead the horse the last few yards to the top of the trail. As soon as he could peek over the edge of the escarpment, he quickly surveyed his surroundings. No Indians. Just more pinions and thicker stands of ponderosa trees. That was worth a sigh of relief and a reassuring pat to the horse on its sweaty neck.

Mounted once more, Bard found himself on a somewhat flat plateau. It took some minutes to orient himself and determine the proper direction he should take to get back on a trail that would lead in the general direction of Fort Wingate.

During the balance of the afternoon there was no sign of Indians. Several times, Bard had to rein the horse around the heads of canyons and deep gulches that had eroded in the mountainous terrain.

Deer were plentiful in the lower reaches. He scattered several small bands of mule deer that were bedded down in the shade of the trees. He was tempted to shoot a small doe, knowing her meat would be tender and easily cooked over a campfire. A second thought canceled the idea. A shot from his Winchester might well bring more Indians.

As he rode, Steve Bard mulled the surprise attack he had experienced. As noted, the Indians did not wear the paint on their faces that invariably announced the northern tribes were looking for trouble. Virtually all of his cavalry experience, and later service as a contract scout had involved the seven bands of what had come to be called the Great Sioux Nation. This tribal confederation spoke three dialects. The Tetons spoke Lakota, the Santees spoke Dakota and the Yanktons had used Nakota until sometime before the Civil War, when they had begun to adopt the Dakota dialect.

Early in his cavalry days as a paroled Confederate, Bard

had learned that these Indians hated the term, Sioux. It had come from the Chippewa term, *nadouessioux*, which translated to "little snakes." These Plains tribes and the Chippewa had been longtime foes. The cavalry tended to think of the pony soldiers as Sioux. It also was recognized that when they were on the warpath, their painted faces, even some of their horses daubed with colors, left no doubts as to what they were about.

Standing on the rim of the canyon and looking back the way he had come, Bard was puzzled. The first shot from the Indians pursuing him had landed several yards in front of his horse. Was the rifleman a poor shot or had the bullet been meant just to spook him? The rider considered the possibility that he had run into a hunting party and the hunters had decided to have some fun with the lone horseman.

Bard shook his head, rejecting that thought. From what had happened, he was certain the Indians had been serious in their attack. He'd been lucky to have escaped.

The sun was low, the orange orb about to drop behind a row of hills in the distance, when Bard spotted what in the distance appeared to be a small settlement. It was located on the side of the mountain ahead of him. As he drew closer, he smelled smoke and a few minutes later was able to make out what was left of half a dozen buildings that had been constructed of peeled ponderosa logs. Most of the logs were marked by fire or totally destroyed by the flames. It was almost an hour and growing dark before he was close enough to read a crude hand-lettered sign that was nailed to a tree: SILVER HILL.

Bard was tempted to take the map out of his saddlebags and see whether the community was marked. He didn't remember seeing any mention of the town when he had inspected the map earlier. It was growing dark, though, and he decided to check the map later.

As he rode into the gathering of burned structures, Bard was struck by the fact that the ponderosa logs that had not been burned were still yellow with the freshness of their appearance. The timbers had not been in place long enough for weather to age them. The community was almost new, but it quickly became obvious it was deserted. There were no signs of people or animals, although one structure had an adjoining corral. The gate bars were down and the enclosure was empty. Tracks showed that shod horses had come through the opening. Pausing beside the corral fence, the horseman bent in his saddle to inspect the piles of horse manure that were visible in the arena. Most of them were relatively fresh. No more than a day old from their appearance. There also were the tracks of unshod ponies and Bard thought again of the Indians that had chased him.

Behind the corral, Bard spotted what he thought to be a cave at first glance, but closer inspection showed it was a man-made shaft. He glanced back to where he had passed the sign. Silver Hill was a mining camp, but the miners had fled.

The horseman dismounted and looped a rein around one of the corral rails, then began to search through the houses. It was evident that some of them had housed women as well as men. In two of the burned structures, he found women's clothing. It wasn't often that miners took their families into the hills with them, but the sign identifying the camp suggested that there had been plans for establishing a permanent community.

In one of the burned structures he found a body. It was that of a woman who looked to be in her late teens. Her dress had been torn off and tossed on a chair. She had been raped, then her head bashed in. Bard gulped at the sight. He had seen similar atrocities on the northern plains, but it was the sort of sight no one was likely to get used to seeing.

He stepped outside and looked about for a likely spot for a grave, but it didn't take him long to discover that there was only a few inches of topsoil covering solid rock. Finally, he moved back into the house, draped the body of the woman in her torn dress and lifted the body in his arms. He judged that she weighed no more than a hundred pounds; maybe less. He carried her past the remains of the other five structures, circling the corral to reach the mineshaft he had spotted earlier. His intention was to deposit the body inside the shaft, then use some of the partially burned timbers to block the entrance against coyotes, bears and other scavengers. He knew it was the best he would be able to do.

Carrying the stiff body in his arms, Bard had to bend his head to enter the mine shaft. The rock ceiling was no more than five feet high. It was dark inside and he paused for a moment, waiting for his eyes to adjust to the dimness.

"Who are yuh, mister?" a gasping voice asked from the darkness. Bard felt a shaft of fear lance through his being. He almost dropped the body.

"Who are yuh?" the voice repeated.

Bard slowly knelt to deposit the body of the girl on the floor of the shaft. Still staring into the darkness, he was able to make out the figure of a man lying on the rock-strewn floor.

"Steve Bard. I'm a government scout. Who're you?"

The reply was a ragged cough followed by a groan. Bard used the matches from his jacket pocket to strike a light. The man lying five feet in front of him had raw blood on his shirt and more blood was seeping from the corner of his mouth. Bard realized the man was only moments from death.

"Who shot you?" he wanted to know.

"Navajos." The reply came in what was little more than a whisper.

Bard shook his head scowling. "They're at peace. On the reservation. Sure it wasn't Apaches or Southern Utes?" Both tribes still were considered hostile.

"Navajos. Didn't think they'd attack us. Me'n my daughter." the man whispered, then began to cough. More blood spewed from his mouth and he attempted to sit up. Instead, his body dropped back, the sound of his skull hitting the rock floor creating a dull, echoing thud.

Bard didn't have to touch him to know the man was dead.

Chapter Three

It was well after dark by the time Bard was able to block the entrance to the mine shaft with timber from the burned buildings, then roll several small boulders from the edge of the building site so they rested against the damaged wood and offered additional protection for the two bodies in the shaft. The best protection, he knew, would be a charge of black powder to blast the tunnel closed, but he had searched the burned-out structures. Had there been any explosives in the mining camp they no doubt had been taken by the fleeing miners or had been appropriated by the raiding Indians.

A three-quarter moon was rising by the time he finished his crude burial efforts and stepped back to survey his work. As nearly as he had been able to tell, the dead miner had been in his forties, but it was the man's daughter that bothered the scout. She had been no more than twenty, he judged. Too young to die the way she had.

As he stood there in the moonlight, Bard noted a familiar sound for the first time. It was the gurgle of running water coming from somewhere on the other side of the settlement. There no doubt were shafts dug by other miners in the area,

15

but the settlement had been built where it was close to water. In that instant, he realized the extent of his thirst and knew that his horse had to be in the same need.

Returning to the corral where he had left the gelding, Bard loosened the reins and led the animal in the direction of the persistent trickling sound. Less than thirty yards from the edge of the camp he found a flat, open area with a small stream running through it. He held the horse's reins as he allowed the animal to drink. When it had its fill and raised its head, Bard dropped the reins, hung his hat on the saddle horn and threw himself on his belly, burying his face in the mountain stream. It was cold and he jerked his head back, shaking the water out of his hair. After a couple of deep breaths, he bent forward to sip from the flowing water.

A badly battered cavalry-issue canteen hung from his saddle and the scout untied it and stepped back to the stream, empting perhaps half a pint of stale water into the stream, then bent to allow the flow to fill the container. As he was strapping the canteen to the saddle once more, he glanced about. The small clearing through which the stream ran had enough grass that he figured his horse could make a meal during the night.

He removed from the saddle the coiled length of the forty-foot braided rawhide *riata*, the working tool of Mexican horsemen, which he had purchased before leaving Santa Fe. He removed the bridle and looped the noose around the animal's neck. The gelding already was chewing at the short grass as Bard stripped off the saddle and the sweat-damp blanket beneath.

Bard dropped the saddle at the edge of the clearing and tied the end of the *riata* to the saddle horn. He spread the saddle blanket in front of the saddle, then fumbled in one of the saddlebags until he found what had the appearance of a large sausage. Actually, it was the pemmican of the Plains tribes, which had been packed in a length of buffalo intestine, then knotted at each end.

Using the long-bladed folding knife he carried in his pocket, Bard sliced off an inch-thick piece of the Indian food, unwrapped the strip of outer intestines, then began to chew the concoction of buffalo meat, nuts and berries that an unknown squaw had packed by hand. Oddly, he had come across the pemmican in a store in Santa Fe. Since the old Spanish town marked the end of what had been the Santa Fe Trail before the railroad arrived, it still was a major trade center and all sorts of strange but useful goods were to be found in the hundreds of shops in the center of the community.

Bard washed down the mixture with water from his canteen, then hung the container back on his saddle. He removed his boots and positioned them near his feet before settling back, his head on his saddle, and pulling half of the saddle blanket over him.

From experienced gained over other nights on the trail from Santa Fe, he had learned that the horse was not likely to move so far as to tighten the noose around his neck. If the animal should do so, the *riata* would pull the saddle on which his head rested. That movement, he knew from long experience, would awaken him instantly.

Bard did not consider himself a particularly religious man, but he did hold the belief that prayer was a positive thing; there were enough negatives in simply trying to stay alive in his line of work. Staring up at the three-quarter moon, he thought about the two bodies he had placed in the mineshaft. A feeling of sadness suddenly swept over him.

He closed his eyes and said a short prayer for the benefit of the two strangers he had entombed. Maybe Someone or Something out there Somewhere beyond the moon and the stars would hear and make an effort to take special care of the pair's departed souls. If not, the prayer still didn't hurt. As he yawned, he silently acknowledged the fact that it made him feel, at least, that he had made some effort.

Bard awoke only once during the night. That awakening came when his horse snorted, apparently sensing some strange creature in the dark nearby. The scout reached out to touch the *riata*, finding there was slack in it. He lay still, listening until the horse began to graze once more. Bard realized there probably were bears or mountain lions in the area, but the horse would have been a great deal more agitated had he smelled the presence of one of those predators. It was after dawn when he awoke and sat up to pull on his worn, cracked cavalry boots.

In a repetition of the previous evening's actions, the scout cut another hunk of pemmican off his roll, consuming it while he watched his horse continue to nibble at the short grass. For the animal, it seemed more a way of passing time than satisfying hunger. He had grazed through most of the night. Done with what had to pass for a morning meal, Bard rose and began to coil the *riata* as he walked toward the horse. He made a twist in the rawhide and slipped it over the horse's nose to effect an adequate halter. With this, he led the animal down to the creek, where it again drank its fill.

As the animal drank, Bard dropped the coil of braided rawhide to the ground, but within easy reach, then refilled his canteen. That done, he again went to his belly to drink upstream from his mount, then came up to his knees to splash water on his face and neck. He stood and wiped the drops away with a bandana he dragged from a hip pocket.

He had just picked up the *riata*'s coils, when he heard the whinny of a horse. His own mount raised its head to reply, but Bard gave a jerk on the makeshift halter and reached up to clamp his hand over the animal's nostrils. Moments later, four men rode into sight on the far side of the burned out mining camp.

"This is the place yuh couldn't find in the dark?" One of them asked, as all four drew up their horses to survey the damage.

"It didn't look like this the last time I seen it," another replied. "Wonder what happened." None of the quartet had yet noticed Bard or his horse.

"Well," announced the first speaker, "probably just as well we camped back there in th' weeds. Hell, yuh can still smell smoke from this stuff. It must've burned just recent-like." He glanced about "And where're the people?"

The other man shook his head, glancing about. "Don't know. There was about a dozen of 'em when I came through before. Miners and some wives. That was six, seven months back about."

The first speaker turned in his saddle to look about. He spotted Bard and his gelding. An ancient cap-and-ball six-gun appeared in his hand.

"They ain't all gone," the man declared. By the time he had finished this announcement, gun pointed at Bard, the scout had his hands elevated, palms toward the new arrivals.

"I'm Steve Bard," was the explanation, offered with what he hoped was a grin. "I camped here last night."

"What're you doin' here, Mr. Bard?" the man with the gun asked quietly. He wore a short beard and in spite of his manner, the muzzle of the revolver did not waver. His eyes were narrowed in suspicion. The other three riders were scowling, awaiting an answer.

"I'm a contract cavalry scout," Bard explained. "I'm on my way to Fort Wingate for a new assignment."

Another bearded rider edged his horse up close to the

man with the gun. He motioned toward the burnt-out buildings. "What happened here?"

Hands still at shoulder level, Bard offered a shrug. "I don't rightly know. I rode in late yesterday and found a dead woman, probably raped b'fore she was killed. There was a mineshaft close by and I took her up there to bury her. Found her pa still alive, but only barely. He said Navajos got them."

He paused to allow his explanation to soak in.

"Yuh can lower your hands, Mr. Bard," the man announced as he holstered his gun. "Anything else yuh can tell us?"

Bard's hands came down, but he was careful to keep his right away from the butt of his Colt six-gun. He shook his head.

"The miner said he didn't think the Indians would attack. I take that to mean the others left here. Maybe went to the fort. He must've stayed to protect his claim. If so, it got him and his daughter killed."

"Where are the bodies?"

Bard waved a hand in the direction of the now blocked mineshaft. "I put them both in th' shaft and closed it off as best I could. Said a prayer for them."

The man who appeared to be the leader of the foursome nodded. "Couldn't hurt none. You say you're headed for a fort?"

"Fort Wingate." Bard turned and pointed in a generally western direction. "It oughta be over there about fifteen, maybe twenty miles near as I can figure. Where you all headed?"

"California," the man declared, "but we didn't bargain for this. We thought all the Injuns were on reservations."

"Officially, most of them are," Bard agreed. "The problem seems to be in keepin' them there!"

The leader edged his horse closer to where Bard stood

and leaned down, extending his right hand. "I'm Tom Howard," he announced, then turned to indicate the other man who had spoken. "This is my cousin, Jim Jensen."

He introduced the other two as Miller and Smith and Bard nodded to each of them in turn, although there had been no first names attached to the introductions. Smith and Miller did not return his nod. They continued to stare at him, still scowling.

"Yuh say Navajos did this?" Howard asked, glancing over his shoulder at the charred ruins.

"Reckon so," Bard admitted on a somewhat reluctant note. "That's what th' miner told me before he died. Yesterday a band of Indians took off after me. I had a tough time shakin' them. I reckon they was Navajos."

The one called Jim Jensen glanced at Howard, then at Bard. "We're not Indian fighters, Steve. We're farmers. Any problem with us tagging along with yuh to this fort?"

Bard offered a grin, shaking his head. "No problem. Five guns are sure better'n one from where I stand. Let me get saddled up!"

Steve Bard was not certain just how accomplished farmers were supposed to be with firearms, but he couldn't help but ponder the draw by Tom Howard that had made the old .36 caliber Navy Colt appear so suddenly in his hand.

Chapter Four

Captain Boyd Jackson sat behind the commanding officer's desk, frowning at the individual standing before him. He nodded to a chair.

"Sit down, Mr. Ransom. I was hoping to see you yesterday."

"I came as soon as I was able, captain." There was no apology in the other man's voice as he deposited his wide-brimmed Mexican sombrero on the edge of the captain's desk and took the seat. He was a big man, over six feet tall and carrying well over two hundred pounds. Most of his weight looked to be solid muscle. His hair was cut short in contrast to the thick drooping mustache that covered his upper lip. If one looked close, a scar was visible beneath the growth. The man had bushy eyebrows that arched above deep-set black eyes.

The captain was noticeably uncomfortable sitting at a colonel's desk and taking on the absent colonel's responsibilities, but tried to hide it as he settled back in the chair.

"Mr. Ransom, as you know, Colonel Byrd has been called back to Washington. That puts me in charge of this post. It also makes me responsible for the welfare of the settlers in this area as well as protecting the fort."

The man named Ransom nodded. "I reckon I understand that. I just don't know what yuh want from me."

"From all the signs and what we hear from our scouts, it looks as though the Indians may be planning to attack this fort. I am officially requesting that you bring your men here to help defend the fort and the civilians who've flooded in here in the past few days."

Ransom stared across the desk at the officer, shaking his head as his lips parted in a cynical smile. "Aren't you over-estimating a few renegade redskins, captain?"

It was the captain's turn to shake his head. "I don't know what's going on. Something has upset the Navajos. They're supposed to be farmers, Mr. Ransom, peaceful farmers, but they're raiding and looting settlers around here. Things are bad enough that a band of them were seen day before yesterday near Silver Hill. The whole mining camp left the diggings and came here for protection. Those people are frightened!"

While the captain was explaining, Ransom had withdrawn a long, black cigar from his inside coat pocket, lighting it with a match that he blew out. He looked about for a place to deposit the matchstick before he simply dropped it on the floor. The silent expression of contempt was not lost on the cavalry officer. Ransom puffed on the cigar, then withdrew it from his mouth, offering a grimace.

"I'm runnin' a cattle and horse ranch, captain. Your army's s'posed to be protectin' my interests, not th' other way around. I can't turn my hands over to army control just because you think there may be danger. They've got work to do." He shook his head again. "If your colonel was here, he'd agree with what I'm tryin' to tell yuh."

Captain Jackson's features hardened and he glared at the man for a long moment before he spoke. "I could declare martial law, Ransom. I could order your men to help in the defense!"

Ransom offered a tolerant smile as he inspected the end of his cigar, then flicked the ash on the floor with a further show of arrogance. "If a green young captain ordered martial law in this country for no good reason, he'd be laughed outa the army, if he wasn't court-martialed first for exceedin' his authority."

The rancher rose abruptly, sweeping his hat off the edge of the officer's desk. "I'm sorry, captain, but I need my men on my ranch. I just don't see any real trouble brewin' with the Injuns as a whole, but there're always a few troublemakers."

As Jud Ransom turned toward the door, the captain came around the end of his desk. He was a step behind the rancher when Ransom paused on the board sidewalk outside the office, staring toward the fort's main gate.

The gate was being swung open by an armed sentry, allowing five horsemen to enter. The riders drew rein, identifying themselves to the sentry. Both officer and rancher watched the event, while Jackson attempted one last plea.

"If it turns out you're wrong, we'll need all the help we can possibly round up. If the Navajos take to the warpath, you'll need us maybe more than we need you, Ransom."

Again, Ransom shook his head, continuing to watch the mounted quintet that had just arrived. There was a puzzled frown on his face. "I'll be happy to come here if there's real trouble, captain, but I have to protect my own interests until that happens. If it ever happens."

Leading the party of five, Steve Bard drew rein on his gelding and pointed to a hitch rack in front of one of the company offices. Led by the man called Howard, the others reined in that direction and dismounted to tie up their horses. The four riders stood close together, looking about the confines of the fort.

"Looks like everybody in the country's come here," the man called Jensen declared. There was no doubting his observation, for the entire parade ground in the center of the fort was covered with wagons, carts, livestock and people. The wagons had been drawn up in a circle, the teams and saddle horses tied outside, but between the wagons one could see men, women and a number of children. Blankets and sheets had been laid out on the hard-packed parade field, some of them under the array of wheeled drayage. It was obvious the civilians were making an effort to make themselves as comfortable as circumstances would permit.

Howard gave the encampment a glance, then shifted his eyes to where Steve Bard had ridden on to where Jackson and Ransom were standing. Bard dismounted and dropped the bridle reins to ground-tie his mount. He turned to face the pair standing on the sidewalk in front of him.

"Captain, I'm Steven Bard, civilian scout. I've been assigned here for duty with your command." He glanced toward the civilian encampment. "I need to talk with yuh, when you're done here."

Jackson eyed the newcomer, noting his rough appearance. "What can I do for you, Mr. Bard?"

"Thought I'd best report how I was jumped by a band of Indians late yesterday. It might've been th' same band that burned th' Silver Hill minin' camp. I buried a man and his daughter up there."

"What kind of Indians were they?" Ransom demanded, causing Jackson to cast him a look of disapproval.

"Mr. Bard reports to me, Ransom," the officer pointed out coldly, his eyes still on the scout.

"I'm more familiar with the tribes up on the Northern Plains, captain, but I'd wager these were Navajos."

Jackson cast Ransom a glance that carried a touch of triumph as he declared, "But the Navajos are peaceful farmers!"

Bard, hearing the irony in the officer's tone, shook his head. "Not the bunch chasin' me, captain. The rifles they was shootin' weren't made from hoes or shovels!"

The cavalry officer turned to the rancher, no longer begging. There was ice in his tone as he spoke. "Mr. Ransom, you'll have to excuse me. Mr. Bard, please come into my office."

Thirty yards away, Kalispell Kane was coming out of the sutler's store, where he had gone to buy tobacco. He was stepping off the board sidewalk that fronted the store, when he glanced toward the captain's headquarters. He froze for an instant, then turned to step quickly to the corner of the building, turning out of sight.

A moment later, he looked around the corner, a Remington revolver clutched in his hand. He raised the handgun, pointing it at Steve Bard. Before he could fire, a big hand came over his shoulder to grab his wrist. Surprised, Kane struggled, unable to see his opponent. Slowly the gun was forced down until it was shoved into his worn holster.

"What th' hell're you doin', Kalis?"

Kane turned to glare at Jack Gentleman, hatred in his tone. "That's Steve Bard. Th' bastard killed my brother! Almost got me, too!"

Kane turned back to look in the indicated direction, but Bard already had disappeared inside the captain's office. Gentleman grabbed Kane forcefully by the shoulder, turning him so they were face-to-face. There was a pitying smile on the big man's lips.

"And you're goin' to shoot him in the middle of a fort full

of armed soldiers!" He shook his head. "You must want to be hanged!"

Kane stiffened at the words, wriggling under Gentleman's grip. "He'll kill me on sight, Jack."

"Then stay outa sight," the larger man ordered. "Mix with the folks in the camp. You're here to watch what's happening." He was struck by a new thought.

"How'd Bard come to kill your kin?"

"He led th' blue belly horse soldiers after us. 'Til then, we had a good thing goin' sellin' rifles to th' Arapahoes."

"Stolen rifles, I assume." Gentleman didn't expect an answer. Instead of looking at the one-time gunrunner, he was staring across the compound. Ransom had walked away to mount his horse and was riding toward the closed gate, when he glanced at the four recent arrivals who were standing at the hitch rail with their own mounts, waiting. Recognition flooded the rancher's face, as he jerked his horse to a halt.

"Frank! Jesse!" he hissed, not wanting to be overheard.

"Keep it down," the leader of the foursome stiffened, glaring at Ransom. "I'm Tom Howard." He growled under his breath. He jerked a thumb to indicate his brother. "This here's Jim Jensen."

Ransom could not suppress a chuckle. "Wouldn't do for that school boy captain to know he has the James brothers right here in his midst, would it?"

For a moment, both of the James brothers glared at Ransom. It was Frank who spoke up, forcing his tone to sound conversational. "That's true, but it'd also be a real feather in that officer's hat if he found one of Quantrill's renegades under his nose. I reckon there's still a price on your head, too." He hesitated for a moment before asking boldly, "What do you call yourself these days?"

"That was a long time ago," Ransom stated. "Things

change. Since coming here, I'm Jud Ransom." He glanced about and saw Gentleman riding out from the side of the sutler's store to join him. He looked back to Frank and Jesse.

"I need to talk to both of you. I'll send someone from the ranch for you tonight."

Both of the brothers were eyeing him with suspicion, evidence that there was little trust, but it was Jesse who offered a nod.

"It don't cost nothin' to talk."

"Tonight then."

Ransom spurred his horse, jerking his head toward Gentleman, who reined his mount, a big dappled gray, to fall in beside the rancher. As they rode toward the gate being opened for them by the sentry, Gentleman looked back to where Frank and Jesse James were talking to their two followers.

"Someone you know?"

"From a long time ago," the rancher admitted. There was an ominous note in his tone that Gentleman accepted as closing the subject.

Jesse and Frank, both scowling, eyes narrowed, turned to watch the pair pass through the gate. Jesse's tone was heavy with cynicism.

"Like he said, times change."

"The last time we seen him, he was sidin' Bloody Bill Anderson at Lawrence, shootin' women and kids," Frank James recalled before he added, "Times may change, but I ain't all that certain about him."

The other two, Clell Miller and Jeb Smith, glanced at each other, exchanging puzzled looks. Both knew that the James brothers had ridden with Quantrill, the looting raider who had posed as a Confederate guerrilla during the War Between the States. Neither had known, though, that Frank and Jesse had been a part of the bloodbath in Lawrence,

Kansas, where Quantrill had once been fired as a school-teacher. The town's male population had been virtually wiped out in that raid.

"You two rode with Bloody Bill Anderson at Lawrence?" Smith wanted to know. There was disapproval in his tone.

Jesse looked at him, shaking his head in a show of open disgust. "We were both in our teens," he declared. "We didn't expect no such slaughter. Me and Frank went home to Missouri after that one."

"Wonder what he wants to talk about," Frank James murmured. Jesse glanced at him.

"Whatever it is, it'll be good for him, probably nobody else! But again, it don't cost nothin' to hear him out." He glanced toward the encampment covering the parade ground.

"We'd best find some place to keep the horses and a spot to bed down our own selves."

Chapter Five

Bard stood at semi-attention before Captain Jackson's desk. Several documents were spread out over the officer's desk, which he continued to peruse, as he spoke.

"These orders tell me you are being sent to us on special detail as a civilian scout, Mr. Bard."

"I didn't know about your trouble with th' Navajos when I signed up again, captain. I figured this would be a nice, quiet tour of duty with all the redskins tendin' their corn and beans. Chances are, though, I may be able to learn more about the reasons for the trouble than one of your professional soldiers."

The young officer looked up, not bothering to cover his annoyance. "Indeed? And what are your qualifications?"

"Several years of scouting for the Seventh Cavalry up in Wyoming, then two years of trappin' with Indians before I signed on to scout, again."

Jackson looked down at the papers once more, spending a moment shuffling them before he found the sheet he wanted.

"It says here you were a captain in the Confederate forces

during the war. You were captured and agreed to parole to fight Indians."

The scout nodded. "That's right. Before I was took prisoner of war, I served under Brigadier General Jeb Stuart."

There was a long pause before the captain looked up to inspect his new scout more closely. "Those of us who fought him know that Jeb Stuart certainly didn't suffer any dullards among his officers." He allowed himself a smile, nodding. "Pull up a chair, captain. General Stuart fought Indians before he resigned to join the Confederacy. We could probably use him now."

Bard glanced toward the chair in which Jud Ransom had been seated earlier and drew it a bit closer to the front of the desk before sliding his haunches onto the wooden seat. Captain Jackson drew a box of cigars from a drawer in the desk, opened it and was shoving the box across the desk.

"General Stuart was only thirty-one years old when he died at Yellow Tavern. The loss of a fine man, Captain Bard. I hope you enjoy a cigar."

"I'm just plain Steve Bard these days, captain." The scout made the statement quietly as he selected a cigar, sniffed its length with appreciation, then bit off the end. He deposited the tip in the ashtray gracing the captain's desk and drew the block of sulfur matches from his shirt pocket.

Captain Jackson also had taken one of his cigars and leaned forward so that the scout could light both cigars on the same match. With ash appearing on each smoke, Jackson leaned back to take another judging look at the man seated across from him.

"If you've been scouting for the United States army, you must realize we tend to do some things quite differently than you did in your Confederate force."

Bard removed the cigar from his mouth and stared at the captain, nodding. There was a note of ice in his reply.

"I'm fully aware of that, captain." There was another moment of silence before Jackson shook his head with a grimace as though to shake off memories of the war in which they had served on opposing sides.

"I know you just got here, Steve, but what do you think about our Indian troubles?"

Bard took a long puff off the cigar, exhaling slowly, seeming to ponder the officer's question before he answered with slow, chosen words.

"Somewhere around here is supposed to be a place called Massacre Mountain. From what I've studied, that's where the Apaches and Navajos had a big battle many years ago. The Navajos were defeated and decided it cost less blood to go to farming. From what I've been told, they're a peaceful people. It takes a lot to stir them up these days."

The cavalry officer heaved a sigh. "A part of Jud Ransom's ranch now covers this place they call Massacre Mountain. Until now, I didn't know why it had that name." He paused, inspecting the dusty trousers and the soiled buckskin shirt before he added, "You've come a long way, Steve."

Bard started to rise. "That's right, sir and the first thing I need besides some hay and a bit of grain for my horse is a bath."

The captain also rose, nodding. "Of course. With all the settlers flooding in here, we had to make an arrangement. Over back of the stables, we've set up a tent around a big horse trough we moved into it. It's a community bath, but there's a section of canvas to separate the men's side from the ladies and youngsters. We try to change the water every day, so it's not too bad, considering the circumstances."

* * *

After finding a stall in the stables, untacking his horse and forking some prairie hay into a manger, Bard glanced about for grain sacks but saw none. With a shrug, he decided to check on it later. Patting his horse on the neck, Bard went looking for the community shower.

Bard found the crude arrangement with little problem and paused to look it over. Just as the captain had described, a canvas fly separated the tent into two sections. One hand-lettered sign indicated the men's side, while a similar sign marked the entrance to the side reserved for women and children. Another placard planted in front of the tent announced: Bring Your Own Soap and Towel

Bard offered a grimace and turned back toward the stable and the saddlebags he had left with his saddle. He didn't have a towel, but he figured he could use an old shirt for drying off.

Inside, the James brothers had just finished bathing in the circular horse tank that was formed from interlocking cedar boards. Frank was buttoning his shirt, while Jesse used a piece of broken mirror attached to a pole in trimming his beard. The gun belts of both men hung from a bent nail pounded into the pole. Finished with his trim, Jesse used a towel to wipe his face and beard. Finished with buttoning, Frank was stuffing his shirttail into his pants.

"I sure wish I knew what Bart Smarten is up to," he muttered. "Based on past knowledge, whatever it is has to be illegal."

On the other side of the canvas partition dividing the tank Lane Lester was submerged in the water. She had been lying so that the back of her head, her hair and her shoulders were soaking. It was her first bath in a number of days and she had been enjoying the minor luxury, lying there with eyes closed. At the sound of the irritation in Jesse James's voice, her eyes opened and she frowned.

Nothing more was said and by the time Steve Bard slipped past the tent flap, the James brothers had buckled on their gun belts and left. Bard quickly unbuckled his own gun belt and hung it and his hat on the nails pounded into a tent pole before stripping off his buckskin shirt. Next came his boots, then the dusty cavalry trousers.

Lane Lester had submerged her body and was half asleep in the soothing warmth of the water when she heard a splash followed by resulting waves that surged across her face. She sat up abruptly, sputtering and wiping water out of her eyes with her fist.

"You bathe like a buffalo, mister!" she snarled in the direction of the dividing stretch of canvas.

"First real bath I've had in two months!" came the cheerful reply.

"You act like it's the first you've ever had!"

That accusation brought a chuckle, more splashing and additional waves. Disgusted, Lane moved to the edge of the tub, scrambled out and reached for her towel.

Now all he has to do is start singing, she thought, offering an unladylike grimace. She was saved from that possibility, however. All that erupted beyond the curtain was more exuberant splashing. She attempted to ignore the sounds as she hurriedly dressed, but at the same couldn't help attempting to picture the ruffian on the other side of the canvas divider. She had known several burly, uninhibited types during the time she had spent at the Silver Hill mining camp. They had shown the same type of disregard for women as her fellow bather. She thought of one in particular, who had a big beer belly, bad teeth and a scraggly beard. It was just as well she was done with her bath, she thought. She certainly wouldn't want to share the water with that man!

Sometime during her dressing, the splashing came to a halt, but she paid little attention as she wrestled with the closures on her high-button shoes. Finally dressed, she looked at her reflection in a sliver of broken mirror, using it to comb her hair.

Lane Lester stood three inches short of six feet, unusual height for a woman, she realized. She was twenty-three years old, a natural blond with green eyes the color of well-handled turquoise. Born in Missouri, where she spent her childhood, she remembered the hatred and plundering of the two sides during the War Between the States. She had grown into a buxom creature who did her best to hide her attributes when in public. She considered her face to be rather plain; her nose was a bit too long for her own liking and there was a strong jaw line that suggested a stubborn streak in her temperament.

Finished arranging her hair as best she could, the woman picked up her towel and other belongings to move toward the entrance that served both sections of the tub. Coming out of the tent and into the coming night, she paused, waiting for her eyes to adjust to the lack of light. Standing there for a moment, she looked around the enclosure of the fort, which covered several acres.

The fort was like others she had seen during her travels with her brother. One side of the rectangle had small adobe and lumber houses that housed officers and their families. At the other end on the parade ground were enlisted barracks and behind that the corral, stables and laundry. A third side of the square had the adjutant's office, the guard house and supply warehouse. The fourth side was where the office and quarters of the commanding officer stood. From the vantage point of his porch, the officer could see most of what was going on within the eight-foot log walls that surrounded the fort.

Lane Lester disliked the fort, mostly because of the crowded conditions that had come about with the miners and settlers in the area taking refuge. She had no friends here and was aware that she was resented by most of the women because of her gambling background with her brother. She was frowning, wondering how long she would have to stay and where she would go when she left. Her thoughts were interrupted by a low whistling sound from behind her. She whirled, the frown becoming a scowl.

The tall man she had seen ride into the fort earlier was standing there, buckling on his gun belt, while he grinned at her. The soiled buckskin shirt he had worn earlier was draped over his shoulder. He now wore a maroon-colored shirt that was dark with water from its use as a towel.

"So you're the one!" Lane's tone verged on a snarl. Her anger at being ostracized by the other women was flaring.

"I always admire a freshly bathed lady, miss." Still grinning, Steve Bard nodded his approval, as he looked her up and down.

"Someone should teach you some decent manners, mister!" she flared. "You near drowned me!"

"You'd better learn to swim, miss."

Lane Lester had her bar of soap wrapped in a flannel washcloth in her right hand, her towel in the other. She hurled the soap at Bard, but it bounced off the canvas wall beside his head. He laughed aloud, as she turned to stalk away from the makeshift bathhouse.

In the growing darkness, Lane moved toward the parade ground where the miners and settlers had set up camp. There was laughter, firelight and the sounds of a guitar. She had the wagon that had been one of her brother's few possessions, but it was parked away from the others. Like the horses of the other settlers, her team was outside the fort, with some of the men taking turns to watch them grazing. It wouldn't do for any of the animals to wander off.

The tall woman knew she was not particularly welcome in

the camp just as she had been shunned by the few women who had lived at Silver Hill with their husbands. She had come to the mining camp with her brother, the two of them planning on opening a saloon. To her brother, it had looked as though Silver Hill would turn into a bonanza. That would mean the few cabins and tents would turn into a boomtown almost overnight. Now, she realized, that hope seemed to be just as dead as her brother. Her brother, Floyd, had run a small game in the mining camp as they had tried to put together enough money to build their saloon. During the past winter, though, Floyd had died of pneumonia and had been buried at the edge of the settlement.

Alone, she had taken over the deck of cards that had been the only thing her brother had left besides the team, wagon and a few old clothes. She had managed to make a bare living as the camp's gambler, incurring the wrath of the few wives in the diggings. It had not taken her long to realize that there never would be enough profit to build any kind of structure. She was not nearly as sharp a gambler as Floyd had been.

As Lane Lester stalked toward her wagon, Steve Bard stood in front of the bathhouse looking after her, while he filled his pipe and lit it. His attention was distracted by action at the main gate, where a sentry was admitting a lone rider. The cavalry scout cast the new arrival a quick glance, then turned his gaze once more to Lane's departing figure.

When the woman disappeared among the wagons, Bard turned to start toward the log structure that housed Captain Jackson's office. The captain had offered to give him a full briefing on the growing Indian problem and what his duties as a scout would entail.

He had gone no more than a dozen steps, when he heard a shot fired somewhere nearby. His first reaction was to drop into a crouch, whirling toward the sound, as he went to the

Colt revolver on his hip. The man who had ridden into the compound was sitting his horse a few yards away, a still-smoking six-gun in his hand.

At the corner of the bathhouse was a body. As the rider dismounted, soldiers came running from several directions. Behind them, buttoning his shirt, was Captain Jackson.

The newly arrived rider had reached the body by the time Steve Bard joined him. The dead man was lying face down, his hand still clutching a black powder percussion Remington revolver. The rider bent to turn the body over so the face was visible. Someone arrived with a coal oil lantern.

"What the hell's going on here, mister?" the captain demanded, stuffing his shirt tail into his uniform trousers.

The new arrival holstered his six-gun before he replied, jerking a thumb toward the body. "This scoundrel was about to shoot this man in the back," he announced, nodding to indicate Steve Bard. "I didn't think that was quite the right thing to do."

"Who are you?" the captain demanded.

"Name's Jim Blade." He glanced at Bard, nodding his head to indicate the body. "You know him?"

Bard was still staring down at the face of the corpse. "I know him. Kalispell Kane. He was caught sellin' stolen army rifles to the tribes up in Wyoming."

"I don't think he liked you much," Blade mused. Bard nodded silent agreement.

"Probably not. I helped to put him outa the gun-runnin' business."

Captain Jackson raised his eyes from the body to stare grimly at the newcomer. "Sir, you are under arrest!"

Chapter Six

The captain whirled as though on springs, seeking out his top enlisted man. "Sergeant major, you will escort this civilian to the guard house immediately!"

The grizzled, white-haired veteran edged forward, the gathered troops parting to make way for him. Jim Blade was staring at the cavalry officer, his expression one of disbelief. "What do you mean? I had to shoot him! Why—"

The captain cut him off, declaring, "There will be an investigation."

"Wait a minute, captain." It was Steve Bard who stepped forward. "You're about to make a total fool of yourself. There is a Federal warrant out for the arrest of Kalispell Kane. Blade here just earned the reward on the man's head!"

Captain Jackson was nonplussed at this turn of events and glanced from Bard to the corpse, uncertain of what should be done, wishing perhaps wistfully that the colonel would return from Washington in the next five minutes. Meantime, Frank and Jesse James had edged into the crowd, trying to get a look at the face of the dead man without attracting attention to themselves.

"We'd better discuss this in my office," Jackson finally decided. He glanced at Bard, then at Jim Blade. "If you two will come with me."

"There's somethin' else the captain should know about Kane," the sergeant major put in.

Jackson glanced at his top soldier and offered a tight nod. "You'd better come along, too, sergeant major."

The sergeant major released his grip on Blade's arm and turned abruptly to the pair of troopers nearest him. "Get a litter and move the body to the morgue."

One of the soldiers moved to where Kane's body lay as though to protect it while the other man stalked away to look for a litter. After a moment, the soldier bent to pick up Kane's hat, which had fallen off during the shooting. He carefully placed the dirty headpiece over the dean man's face. The onlookers began to drift away, as Bard, Blade and Sergeant Major Seth Keene followed Jackson toward his office.

Jesse and Frank James, who had been watching, took a step closer to look down at the man.

"Wonder what that was all about?" Jesse pondered. Frank shook his head, as the body was carried away.

"I've never seen him before," he muttered. "I got a good look at him though."

"I don't know him neither," Jesse agreed.

"One of you named Howard?" A harsh voice demanded. At the sound of the name, Jesse and Frank both turned to face Jack Gentleman, who had ridden through the gate during the post-death excitement. Dismounted, he still held his horse by the reins. Jesse James offered a nod.

"I'm Tom Howard. Ransom sent you?"

Bard and Blade both stood before the desk of the fort's commanding officer, while Jackson sat looking up at them.

Sergeant Major Keene stood in the background in the parade rest position, feet apart, arms behind his back. The captain was frowning at what he was hearing.

"We chased him and his brother over half of Wyoming after they stole rifles from the armory and sold them to the tribes. They'd also been sellin' whiskey to the Arapahoes," Bard stated. "I managed to shoot his brother during the chase, but Kalispell got away. I never knew where he went 'til now."

"But why would he follow you here, Steve?" the officer wanted to know.

Bard offered a shake of his head, frowning. "I think he's probably been here for a time. There's no better way to cause Indian trouble than to get them liquored up on firewater!"

"Captain, may I speak, sir?" the sergeant major asked, tone bright and hard despite his years.

"What it is it, sergeant major?"

"Me and a couple of troopers've had our eye on Kane," the old soldier stated. "He's been doin' chores for the sutler, but that ain't been enough for his food and liquor."

"What're you getting to?" Jackson demanded, frowning.

"Remember them twelve uniforms that ended up missin' from supply? We're right sure, sir, it was Kane who stole them."

The captain shook his head in open puzzlement. "Why would someone steal a dozen uniforms?"

The old soldier offered a shrug. "Maybe someone wanted hisself to have what looked like a squad of soldiers, captain. That's my thought."

Bard reached to his pocket and drew out the leather bag that looked to be a tobacco pouch. The pouch was open, since the scout had inspected the contents on the walk to the captain's office. He balanced the pouch on his palm, an iron-ic smile touching his lips.

"This could tell us somethin', captain. Kane was carryin' it. Must've fell out of his pocket when he went down."

"What is it?" The captain obviously resented the drama Bard was attaching to his discovery. The scout leaned forward to pour five nuggets out on the officer's desk. The bits of gold, one the size of a walnut, reflected their rough sheen in the dim light from the coal oil lamp cornered on the officer's desk.

"There's maybe your reason, captain!"

Captain Jackson stared at the gold nuggets spread out before him, scowling. His expression was one of distaste at the sudden appearance of the brilliant mineral, foreseeing the problems it could create. Word of a gold rush would bring hordes of treasure hunters and the Indians besides the Navajos would fight to protect their lands once again. An old, old story. After several seconds, he heaved a sigh and settled back in his chair, eyeing Jim Blade.

"And what's your part in all this?" he wanted to know. Blade returned his stare boldly. He offered a shrug.

"I guess I'm a semi-innocent bystander," he declared. "I just happened along when that renegade was trying to bushwhack this gent." Blade nodded to indicate Bard. His frown deepening, Jackson was on the point of speaking, when Bard leaned across his desk once more.

"He probably saved my life, captain."

The young officer glanced from one to the other, his frown hardening into a full-scale scowl as his eyes went back to the nuggets lying on his desk.

"Keep your mouths shut about this. That includes you, sergeant major. Talk to no one. With the colonel gone, I don't need a gold rush coupled with an Indian uprising. We've already got enough problems just trying to feed that bunch of civilians out there camped on our parade ground!"

* * *

On the Ransom ranch, lights were lit in two rooms of the ranch house as Jack Gentleman reined his horse in before a hitch rail and swung out of the saddle. The James brothers followed his example to stand looking about uncertainly.

"He's come a long way from Lawrence, Kansas," Frank James muttered under his breath. Gentleman may have heard the observation, but motioned that the two were to follow him.

"Mr. Ransom's waitin' for you," he announced.

Gentleman led the pair up a gravel path to the door of the ranch house, which appeared to be built from unpainted rough-cut lumber. He opened the front door and motioned them in. Frank and Jesse entered and Gentleman shut the door behind them.

Inside the house, the pair found themselves in a hallway that had doors on each side, obviously leading to the rooms. One door was open with light coming from it.

"Frank? Jesse? Is that you?" came a call from the room. "Come on in."

The man who called himself Jud Ransom was seated at a roll-top desk, a stack of documents in front of him. He rose and extended his hand toward Jesse. There was a moment of hesitation before the noted train robber shook it. When Ransom extended the hand toward Frank, there was a little less reluctance to go through the ritual of friendship and mutual respect.

"Good of you boys takin' the time to come," Ransom stated, offering a smile. He motioned toward a leather-covered sofa that was at a right angle to his desk. "Just take a seat there."

Jesse was staring at Ransom thoughtfully, while his brother looked about the room. It was well-furnished and in a rock fireplace, a ponderosa log was burning with a brightness that cast odd shadows against the walls.

"How about a cigar?" Ransom asked. He was dressed

somewhat formally, wearing a long broadcloth coat. He took three cigars from an inside pocket and extended one to each of the two men sitting across from him. He then rose and went to the fireplace, where he found a twig and held it under the flames of his own smoke for an instant.

"Days like this make me realize how much time has passed and how rapidly it has disappeared," Ransom declared thoughtfully as he turned to hold the burning twig beneath the tip of Jesse's cigar, then lit the stogie Frank held between his own lips.

"It's been a long time since the old days," he added, eyeing the ash on the end of his stogie. He dropped back into the chair, surveying the brothers with a slight smile. Jesse was still staring at him, while Frank seemed more relaxed.

"Everyone thought you was with Quantrill, when th' Union soldiers caught him in that barn and shot him." Jesse's words were almost accusatory.

Ransom flicked an ash off his cigar onto the stone floor, pursing his lips as though trying to decide how to reply to the statement that amounted to an accusation.

"No," he said slowly. "I wasn't with Bill when that happened."

Frank was inspecting the ash on the tip of his own cigar. "There was some folks figgered you gave Quantrill away to save your own hide."

Ransom's attitude did not change in spite of the accusation, but it was apparent he was choosing his words with care.

"Th' war was over and we'd lost." He hesitated before adding quietly, "Let's just say I saw the light and changed sides."

During the rancher's speech, Jesse seemed to tighten up, sitting higher in his chair. He suddenly leaped to his feet, jerking his Navy Colt free of its holster.

"You yellow-gutted bastard!"

"Jesse! Don't! You'll die!" Ransom's tone was sharp and he glanced toward the glass window at the end of the room. There came the sound of metal tapping on the glass and both Frank and Jesse turned to look in that direction. On the other side of the transparent pane, Jack Gentleman stood with a six-gun in each hand, the blackness of the night serving as a background.

Ransom's tone was conversational as he stated, "He'll kill you. He'd like being the man who killed Jesse James."

There was a long moment of hesitation before Jesse lowered his gun, then shoved it back into its holster. He slowly retook his seat beside his brother, his earlier stare now a glare of open dislike.

"Why'd you want to see us, Jud?" he demanded.

Ransom had seemed amused at the interplay between Jesse and his own gunman, but suddenly he was all business, leaning forward to return Jesse's glare.

"I now why you're in New Mexico Territory, Jesse. You had that little ranch over in Texas and thought you was out of the train robbin' and bank holdups. Then you heard there was a Texas Ranger on your trail."

Jesse shook his head. "The Texas ranch is still mine, Jud, and nobody's chasin' us. Me'n Frank are doing somethin' for our ma. We're headed for California to try to find our daddy's grave. He died out there durin' the Gold Rush."

Ransom leaned back in his chair once more, offering a shrug. "Well, maybe it's time you boys cooled off, but believe me, there really is a ranger lookin' for you both. Maybe my sources of information are better than yours."

"Our fame seems to precede us even here," Frank observed on a note of irony that Ransom ignored.

"How're you boys fixed for cash?" Ransom wanted to

know. Jesse bristled at the question, but Frank put a calming hand on his arm. "We left in sort of a hurry," he admitted. "We was thinkin' of maybe visitin' a couple of banks along th' way."

"Banks are few and far between out here," Ransom told him. "And most of them don't have much money in them. Looks to me like you need a place to hole up for a time. If we can make a deal, you all can go on to California in a few weeks with some respectable cash."

Jesse, still glaring at the rancher, shook his head. "One don't live long in our business by runnin' around blindfolded, Jud."

Ransom leaned across the desk, his amused attitude gone. His features hardened as he spoke. "This law they're calling the Homestead Act will bring thousands of new settlers into this area. They're already movin' in."

"And you don't want them here," Frank added with knowing thoughtfulness.

Ransom offered a quick nod. "Massacre Mountain and what's all around it is mine! I aim to keep it."

"And you're hirin' a batch of gun slicks like Jack Gentleman to keep them homesteaders out," Jesse ventured.

Ransom offered a chuckle that was not reflected in the harshness of his expression. "The Indians'll keep them out. My men just help out a bit. I have several bands of renegade redskins I can organize under a warrior named Long Arm ready to attack the fort on my say-so. He wants those new repeating rifles."

"With that kind of rifle, they could make life miserable for the army for years," Frank declared.

"That's the idea," Ransom admitted, "but I can use your help for a time."

Jesse rose carefully from his chair, shaking his head with a frown.

"We seen one massacre, Jud. Lawrenceville. I don't reckon we want to be involved in another."

There was a touch of contempt in the rancher's tone as he spoke. "You don't have much choice, Jesse. Here you have asylum. I'll be able to protect you. Otherwise. . . ." Ransom ended his comment with a shrug.

"You'd turn us in?" Frank rose from the sofa to stand beside Jesse.

"He turned in Bill Quantrill, didn't he?" Jesse rasped. Ransom ignored the remarks of both men.

"Gentleman will show you to the bunkhouse. In the morning, we can send for those other men you left back at the fort."

Frank James was slower to anger than his younger brother, but he stared at Ransom with an expression that could only be interpreted as contempt coupled with loathing.

"Better watch your back, Ransom, or you'll find a bullet in it."

Ransom offered a knowing smile at the same moment the click of a door latch sounded.

"Jack Gentleman covers my back quite well. He'll show you to the bunkhouse."

When the James brothers turned toward the door, Gentleman was there, leaning against the doorframe, a mocking smile on his lips.

Chapter Seven

"I'm sorry, Miss Lester, but it's totally impossible. I just can't do it," Captain Jackson stated as he escorted the woman to the board sidewalk outside of his office. "I hope you understand why."

Lane Lester was frowning as she nodded acceptance. "I understand, but it doesn't help my situation at all."

"You really don't belong in this country, if I may say so," the officer announced. He made a point of not looking at her. He stared out across what had been his parade ground before the settlers had moved in. "You must have some people somewhere who could help you get back East."

"No one. Since my brother died, I've been on my own."

The officer heaved a sigh. "Let me give this some thought. There may be something around here that would be of help." He turned to glance at the office door, where a sergeant stood waiting. His tone took on an official note.

"You'll have to excuse me, miss, but there are several matters that need my immediate attention."

"Certainly," Lane had been dealing with men long enough to know when she was being dismissed. "Go ahead with your business, captain." There was a note in her voice that could have been a combination of hurt and bitterness.

As he turned to re-enter his office, Jackson was wondering whether he should include any mention of the interview with the woman in his next report. After a moment's thought, he decided against it. His refusal to allow her to legalize gambling on the post was in strict keeping with military regulations and, as such, was nothing more than a housekeeping detail. Higher headquarters certainly wouldn't be interested in whether a woman wanted to gamble with the soldiers of his command. Frankly, he thought, she had a lot of gall even to approach him, but he also recognized the fact that people tended to do strange things when verging on desperation. He shook his head with a frown, reminding himself that he had more problems than the welfare of one woman. The report by Sergeant Major Keene regarding missing cavalry uniforms was among his worries. What possible reason could that dead man, Kane, have had for stealing them, if he really was the thief?

Lane Lester was walking away from the captain's office, when she saw that ill-mannered scout, Steve Bard, and the man who had ridden in last night and killed a man before he ever got off his horse. Someone had told her his name was Jim Blade. She paused, watching as they rode through the fort's open gate. She noted that Bard, the Indian scout, had what appeared to be a thick bedroll tied behind his saddle. She watched until the armed sentry swung the heavy gate shut behind the riders.

Lane knew that Blade apparently had saved the scout from a back-shooter the previous evening, but she felt that he and Bard made a strange pair. Her brief contact with the scout told her he was rough and short on tact as well as lacking decent manners. She hadn't met Jim Blade, but he appeared to be more genteel; a man who dealt with thought instead of guns. Then she remembered last night's shooting and shook her head. There was just no telling about men! She was angry at the embarrassment she had experienced as the captain had explained to her why he couldn't allow her gambling enterprise on his post. She had placed a lot of hope in her proposition and she knew Simon Westphal, who operated the civilian-run sutler store, would be disappointed, too. He was always looking for additional sources of income. Selling whiskey to soldiers who made twelve dollars a month was never going to make anyone wealthy!

She had been seventeen when her parents died. The horse drawing their carriage had run away and the couple had been dumped in an ice-strewn river and drowned. Her brother had returned home to Iowa to bury their mother and father, then had taken his younger sister under his wing. In time, she became an important part of his gambling operation.

Floyd Lester was proud of the fact that he was able to make a reasonable living with a deck of cards without cheating, but he taught his sister, blooming into the beauty of full adulthood, to play a role as his assistant. Whenever he was in a big game, she often acted as the dealer so Floyd, her brother, could not be accused of stacking the deck by the losers. If someone in the game objected to her dealing, she simply hung around to watch the game. She had not thought of herself in those days as beautiful, but Floyd explained that her looks and demeanor were enough to provide a definite distraction to the other players. That kind of an edge could help him win.

That had started six years ago. Now she was twenty-three and knew little except cards. With Floyd gone, she had been dealing cards in the wagon camp, but some of the wives were becoming increasingly irritated over the fact that she was taking their husband's money; there was little enough of it and considering the circumstances, none to spare for such costly foolishness as the turn of a card.

The woman gambler recognized the animosity that was growing toward her. As a result, she had approached Simon Westphal, whose small store was of some benefit to local settlers, but was there primarily for the fort's soldiers and their families.

Westphal's establishment supplied military and personal comfort items ranging from bar soap to boot polish and leather thongs for repairing saddles and bridles, but there also was a small bar, where the fort's soldiers could meet at night to drink a beer or two and exchange views on the day's happenings. The beer was shipped in barrels from Santa Fe and it often ran out before a new supply could be brought the distance by supply wagons.

Simon Westphal, Lane had discovered, offered no objections to her running a game in his bar, if he got a ten percent rake-off of her winnings and was not committed to cover any losses. The only problem, he had explained, lay in the fact that his was a government-contracted operation meant only to supply daily needs and liquor to the troops. The gambling in the bar would have to be approved by Captain Jackson.

The sutler had told her he would take it up with the captain, but Lane had suggested she approach the commanding officer instead.

She was hoping that a woman looking to support herself, coupled with a few smiles, might have a positive effect on the captain's decision. She was aware that there were rules against the troops gambling within the fort, but everyone knew it still was going on. Her approach to Captain Jackson had been that it would be better for the troopers to gamble in a semi-controlled situation than rolling dice behind a corral.

Jackson, she learned during her interview, went strictly by the book. As a relatively young officer holding down a colonel's billet on a temporary basis, he was not going to break or even stretch any rules.

Lane Lester decided to wait until later to tell the sutler she had been unable to sway the captain to accept her plan. She also wondered what Captain Jackson had meant about there possibly being something she could do to earn money. She offered a sigh. It probably would be something like work in the fort's laundry, washing soldiers' sweat-encrusted long johns, dirty socks and whatever else they wore!

Her thoughts turned to the two men who had ridden out of the fort minutes before and she found herself wondering what Steve Bard was really like beneath his rough exterior. She sniffed at the idea that she should be interested and lengthened her stride toward the encampment, head held high.

On the trail, Bard and Blade rode side-by-side. For the first half-mile or so, nothing was said. Finally, Blade cast the other rider a questioning glance.

"Where're we headed, Steve, or are we just exercising the horses?"

Bard was silent for a moment, staring down the trail ahead of them. He had been surprised when Blade had asked if he could ride along for the day. He didn't know what the man was up to, but the scout realized the other man's shot of the previous evening probably had saved his life. When he replied, his words were careful, measured.

"According to Captain Jackson, this man, Ransom, refuses to admit there's any Indian trouble around here."

That brought a shrug from Blade. "If he doesn't want to believe it that would seem to be his problem, wouldn't it?"

Bard shook his head. "There's something that just don't

set right." He glanced at the other rider, a questioning frown on his features.

"What're you doin' out here, Blade? You're from back East, ain't you?"

"It's been a long while since I've been there. I never went back after the war ended." He hesitated before adding, "West Virginia. I served with the Union."

There was no apology in his tone. Everyone was aware that Abe Lincoln and his Congress had created the new state from that section of the State of Virginia that had refused to secede from the Union and join the Confederacy. Blade's simple statement of fact brought a shrug from the scout, with a nod of philosophical acceptance.

"I reckon we all had to be on one side or t'other. But what are you lookin' for out here?"

"I'm a journalist," Blade replied after a long pause. "I write things for newspapers, sometimes for magazines like *Harper's Weekly*." He was looking at Bard as they rode, awaiting his reaction.

"That's why you asked if you could come along with me?" Bard was puzzled at the idea. "You thought we might kick up some excitement you could write about?"

Blade nodded. "That's part of it, I suppose. Actually, I'm interested in learning more about this country. What goes on here." He cast the scout a glance. "I figured I'd be best off with someone who knew what goes on."

"I don't know what's happening. I just got here, too."

"But you know about Indians," Blade insisted. That brought a shake of Bard's head.

"Not all Indians. Different tribes have different beliefs, different customs. I know somethin' about the Sioux, the Comanche, the Arapahoe and maybe less about some others, but the Navajos and Apaches around here're a whole different ball of wax. From what I've been told, they don't even think the same as the tribes I've had dealin's with."

There was a long moment of silence before Jim Blade glanced at the scout with a slight grin. "Then maybe we'll learn stuff together. Where are you from, Steve?"

"Corpus Christi. I was a seaman before th' war started."

"You didn't go back to that?"

Bard shook his head. "No reason. My father and two brothers had been using their boat to run guns in for the South. The boat got sunk and they all got killed. By the time my parole to fight Indians for the Union was up, Yankee carpetbaggers was runnin' Texas."

The scout didn't feel he knew the other well enough to explain that when he had returned to the Texas city for only a few days, he quickly found that those he had considered his friends before the war were calling him a traitor for accepting the Union's parole. That included the woman he had been engaged to marry before he had enlisted in the Confederate cavalry. Corpus Christi truly had nothing to offer that he wanted.

During his parole, he had come to respect the Union army and had returned to it. In spite of his varying assignments from one military post or fort to another over the past nine years, he had come to think of the army as his home.

"If we spot a couple of deer or even an elk, we're supposed to take it," Bard declared in a change of subject. "Captain Jackson's worried about bein' able to feed that horde at the fort. Any meat we bring back he'll turn over to them. He told me it'll be some weeks before a military supply train gets down here and there won't be much extra even then for all those folks. What with the trouble, there's no tellin' when that sutler'll get resupplied."

"How long does he think this Indian trouble might last?" Blade wanted to know.

"He don't have any idea. Me neither. He's still trying to learn what' riled up the Navajos. They were real trouble till Sixty-two, when Colonel Kit Carson and th' army took time out from th' war to round them up and walk th' whole tribe to a place near Fort Sumner. Carson wanted to make farmers out of them.

"The tribe finally signed a treaty in Sixty-eight and they was allowed to come back here and take up reservation livin'. According to the captain, 'til just recent times, they've been runnin' a few cattle, herdin' sheep and raising corn and beans, living in peace."

"The captain seemed somewhat put out over the sergeant major's announcement about the missing uniforms," Blade stated. "You have any thoughts on that?"

Bard shook his head. "During the war, I heard stories about how some of them Indians from Oklahoma that joined the Union Army would take rebel uniforms from dead soldiers and wear them to infiltrate the Rebel lines at night. I never did find anyone that knew it to be a fact, though."

Blade chuckled. "Strange. I heard the same thing about the Indians who fought on the Confederate side! I was never able to find anyone who really knew about it, either."

Bard spurred his mount into a gentle canter and Blade did the same to hold his position abreast of the scout. The rocky mass known as Massacre Mountain loomed several miles ahead.

Chapter Eight

The James brothers, Frank and Jesse, were dressed in Union cavalry uniforms that were a poor fit, but unmistakable. The uniforms were complete, except for the lack of issue cavalry boots and gun belts. Instead, the Missouri fugitives wore the flat-heeled farmer boots that were their regular attire and the belts, holsters and six-guns surrounding their waists were their own.

Flanking the pair, Clell Miller and Jeb Smith both were dressed in the same fashion. The foursome looked uncomfortable in the uniform of the force that once had been a sworn enemy. None of their saddles were of the flat-seated design issued to cavalrymen. Each of the outlaws rode his own horse and personal saddle.

Jack Gentleman sat his sorrel stallion, facing the foursome, an ironic smile creasing his lips. Dressed in his usual garb, he shook his head as he eyed the quartet.

"None of you'd ever pass a proper military inspection, but that ain't so important right now."

"This doesn't make much sense," Jesse James declared.

"Why don't Jud Ransom use you and the rest of his gun hawks for this kind of work?"

"It looked like maybe he was gonna have to do that," Gentleman added, "but then you four came along. The Injuns hereabouts know most of us. They'd possibly recognize us unless we wore fake beards and rode unbranded horses. This makes it a batch easier."

Gentleman seemed to be enjoying himself, directing the efforts of such notorious characters as the James brothers. He turned in the saddle to wave toward the crest of a low hill perhaps two hundred yards away.

"Right over that rise is a Navajo watchin' about fifty head of steers."

"I thought these Injuns raised sheep," Clell Miller said, frowning at Gentleman. It was obvious he didn't like the gunman. Gentleman offered a nod of his head.

"That's mostly true, but these steers are part of the tribes' quarterly food allotment from the government. They're tryin' to get them fattened up a bit before they slaughter them."

"Doesn't Ransom have enough cows without robbin' some poor Indians?" Jesse James wanted to know. That brought a tolerating smile to Gentleman's lips.

"Ransom sold them to the army as tribal food rations. Now he's gonna take them back. They're all still wearing his brand."

"The blue coats take blame for the steal and that helps to keep the Navajos mad at the army. Is that it?" Frank James wanted to know.

"That's the general idea," Gentleman agreed. "One thing, though. Don't kill the Injun. Ransom wants him to get back to his people. Tell them how the United States Cavalry soldiers stole their food!"

Jesse James cast Gentleman a look that reflected obvious dislike, but it went ignored by the gunman, if the gun hawk noticed at all. He waved toward the top of the rise.

"Best get a move on. Ransom wants them cows mixed in with his own herd before night time."

He turned to ride away, as Frank and Jesse reined their mounts and rode toward the top of the hill, the other two gang members falling in behind them. Reaching the crest of the hill, Jesse pulled up his mount and the others lined up abreast of him. Below, a lone Navajo—a lad who could be no more than fifteen—was watching half a hundred steers that grazed quietly on the yellowing bunch grass.

"Why're we doin' this, Jesse?" Clell Miller wanted to know, eyeing the herd below. "We're supposed to be on our way to California."

"If we don't do it, we might find the whole New Mexico cavalry on our tails for the reward on us," Jesse James replied, a note of bitterness in his tone.

"This Ransom fellah would turn you in?" Miller sounded as though he didn't believe it.

"You don't know him. If it served his purposes, he'd lynch his own mother," Frank James announced. "We have to go along for right now."

Clell Miller heaved a sigh reflecting his reluctance. "Reckon we'd best get at it then."

"Remember what Gentleman said," Jesse James instructed. "Don't shoot the Indian."

"What if he shoots back?" Jeb Smith wanted to know.

"From here, it don't look like he's armed. Not even bow an' arrow," Frank James put in. "He's just a kid."

"We chase him off and head the cows back toward where Gentleman's waitin'," Jesse ordered, drawing the revolver from his holster. "Let's go!"

Oddly, the four were shouting Confederate war cries as they

thundered down the hill, firing in the air. The young Indian whirled his horse to meet the oncoming attackers. Surprised, it took him only a moment to realize he was in trouble. His remedy was to whirl the little pinto he rode and kick the animal in the heels with his moccasin-clad feet. He was bending low over the horse's neck as he raced down the valley.

Meantime, the cattle were surprised and frightened by the sudden uproar and some of them started to run, following the young Indian.

"Get around them! Cut them off!" Jesse James shouted and spurred his horse to a dead run, the six-gun still clutched in his hand.

The counterfeit cavalrymen raced after the herd, slowly overtaking the lead animals but only after the steers had passed over another hill. Riding at the head of the charging animals, Jesse James managed to change loaded cylinders on his percussion revolver, then began firing once more. Ahead of them, there was no sign of the Indian youth.

It took perhaps ten minutes to turn the herd and get the heaving animals halted. As the four riders slowly bunched the bovines and headed them back the way they had come, Clell Miller glanced at the one nearest to him. Its flanks were still heaving and it was snorting a spray from its nostrils.

"That little run worked off 'bout a week of grazing fat," he ventured, his words those of a farmer who was familiar with livestock.

Less than two miles away, Steve Bard and Jim Blade, riding through a narrow canyon, had heard the firing and pulled up their mounts, staring ahead.

"Sounds like open warfare," Blade ventured, eyes slitted against the bright sun. Bard was staring straight ahead, eyes also narrowed.

"Pistol fire," the scout announced. "None of it's heavy

enough for rifles. Must be more than one person shootin', though. We'd best take a look."

Bard spurred his horse to a ground-covering gallop, Blade following his lead. A sudden pistol shot kicked up dust in front of Bard's horse and he reined it in so rapidly that the animal reared, pawing the air. Blade was able to bring his own mount to a halt without such an effort.

Jack Gentleman rode out from behind a huge boulder that edged the confines of the canyon. His reins were in his left hand, a six-gun in his right. Bard still was trying to calm his prancing mount, but Blade saw the rider and slowly raised his hands, reins clutched in his right fist.

"Hold it right there!" Gentleman shouted. In that instant, Bard spotted him. After a moment's consideration, he also raised his hands.

"You two seem in an all-fired big hurry," Gentleman stated conversationally. In spite of the fact that his tone was almost genial, the muzzle of the gun did not waver.

Steve Bard jerked his head to indicate the mouth of the canyon ahead. "We heard shots comin' from up there."

"Just some of my boys cleanin' out a wolf pack. They've been killin' our young calves."

"Must have been quite a pack," Bard ventured, doubt in his tone. "A lot of gunfire."

"Yeah. A lotta wolves, too," Gentleman agreed, voice taking on a harsh note. "Now you two had best stay back of the property line."

"This is Navajo reservation!" Bard declared. That brought a shake of the head from the man holding the revolver.

"No, it ain't. The reservation starts up ahead about two miles." Gentleman turned to swing his gun muzzle toward a hand-painted sign at the edge of the cleft through the rocks. It appeared to be quite new and read: RANSOM RANCHO KEEP OUT OR GET SHOT!

"We've had some problems with cow thieves of late, so Mr. Ransom don't take kindly to strangers these days."

Jim Blade was on the point of speaking, but Bard pulled back his horse, glancing at the journalist.

"Come on, Jim. Never argue with a gun that's pointed at you."

Bard swung his horse about and started back down the canyon. After a moment, Blade, a scowl still creasing his features, followed. Jack Gentleman grinned as he holstered the six-gun and sat watching the pair retreat in the direction from which they had come. He knew that the James gang would be driving the stolen cattle through the canyon in short order to get them onto Ransom property. Just wouldn't do for others to see what was going on.

After riding through a bend in the canyon, Steve Bard drew rein to took look back, scowling. Jim Blade reined in beside him. The walls of the canyon were lower and ahead they could see open range.

"Why didn't you just tell him we were on the way to see his boss?" Blade wanted to know.

"We'll be back," Bard promised, "but right now, I find that smoke back there somewhat interesting."

He nodded his head to indicate the direction from which they had come. Blade turned to look in the same direction. In the sky above the rim of the canyon, several miles away, puffs of dark smoke were rising one after the other.

"I don't get it," Blade admitted. "Can you read those puffs? Know what they say?"

Blade shook his head. "Maybe if they was Lakota or Cheyenne, but they ain't." He cast a crooked grin at his companion. "But I for certain don't know of any wolves smart enough t'use smoke signals. I don't reckon our friend with the gun does, either."

Chapter Nine

"Sorry, Lane, but that's 'bout how I figured he'd handle it," Simon Westphal muttered. He was hunched over a stack of Navajo-made blankets that had been brought into the fort by some of the squaws from the reservation. He had found a ready market for them among the wives of the fort's officers and a few of the senior enlisted men bought them occasionally, shipping them back to families in the East.

The blankets were woven by hand from the wool taken from the tribe's sheep, then colored with dyes made from local nuts, flowers and other natural resources. The blankets he was not able to sell at the fort, the sutler sent to Santa Fe. From there, they were railroaded east to Kansas City, Chicago and even New York. It seemed those who had never been west of the Ohio River were quick to acquire items of beauty made by Indians. The blankets apparently made great conversation pieces.

"What do you mean?" Frowning, Lane Lester was standing on the other side of the stack of blankets. Westphal shook his head, not looking up from his evaluations of the various pieces of hand-loomed goods.

"Captain Jackson operates strictly by the book, Lane. He ain't gonna make any decisions that might harm his promotion chances no matter how good it might be for th' civilians he's here to protect!"

"You thought he'd refuse my proposition," Lane Lester charged, suddenly angry. "You thought that all along!"

The sutler looked up, a wry smile tilting his lips. He shook his head. "Not all together, ma'am. I thought maybe a few soft words and a pretty face might have some positive effect. He's been out here alone for a long time!"

"You were using me, Simon," came the accusation. That brought another shake of the sutler's head.

"I reckon we was usin' each other. Too bad it didn't work."

"Thanks a lot!" the woman snarled at him, turning on her heel and making for the door.

Outside the store, Lane stood on the wooden sidewalk for a moment, taking deep breaths, attempting to put her anger and disappointment aside. She felt dirty at the way she had been used by the sutler. When she had worked with her brother that was family. She was glad it hadn't worked out. She didn't like the greedy little man. Ignored, of course, was the fact that the approach to Captain Jackson had been her own idea.

The sun was shining brightly and singing from the settlers' encampment spread across the fort's parade ground. Usually, she enjoyed the songs that were sung to pass the time, but at that moment, she hated what she was hearing. They always were songs of hope and cheer, but as she stood there, glaring in the direction of the melded voices, she felt neither emotion.

Worse, she felt she had made a fool of herself with both Westphal and Captain Jackson, in coming up with what apparently was a legally impossible scheme. Both men had recognized it as such. She was particularly angry at Westphal for sending her on a fool's errand that he knew could not succeed! He had allowed her to cheapen herself! Standing there in the afternoon sun, she slowly came to realize that when one is in desperate straits, one tends to take unpleasant measures. Out of that situation, crazy ideas for survival are born.

After several minutes, the blond woman heaved a sigh. She felt like crying, but she wasn't going to. There still were things that had to be done. She had washing to do in the laundry shed. It should be relatively empty by now, since most of the women tended to do the family laundry early in the morning.

She stepped off the board sidewalk to head across the enclosure to the encampment, but was halted by the sound of someone calling her name.

"Miss Lester! Lane Lester!"

She halted and turned her head to see Captain Jackson approaching her from his office. She took a stride as though to continue on, but he called, again, "Wait, Miss Lester!"

She stopped and waited, scowling. What did he want? Was he now going to ban her from the fort for breaking his gambling rules in the encampment?

Lane was still scowling as he approached, but noticed the officer was smiling. Was there a chance he had changed his mind? That he was going to go along with the gambling program she had suggested? There was that belief born of desperation rising once more. This time, she recognized the emotion and its dangers. She waited until the fort commander was only a few feet from her and came to a halt. "You wanted something, captain?" Her scowl had been reduced to the dimensions of a frown, but her question was formal and rather chilly. She still was hurting from his strict military decision.

"I need to talk to you, miss."

"Really? Which of your regulations have I broken?"

He shook his head, still smiling. "None, miss. There's something you can do for all of us, if you will. We have a small morale fund here and I want to pay you to organize a party."

"Because I've worked in saloons, I should be able to cater a party? How flattering!" Lane realized that the anger she had put down moments earlier was starting to grow once more. She didn't like the anger but it was there. "What kind of party?"

The captain's eyes were still on her, but he waved an arm in the direction of the civilian encampment.

"We're so crowded here. I thought a dance and maybe a steak dinner might improve the morale of my own men as well as that of your settlers."

"They're not my settlers, captain. They're your settlers and I doubt that any of the women would come to my party!" She was unable to keep the bitterness out of her voice. The officer took a step that brought him closer and he looked into her face. His smile was gone, replaced by a look of concern.

"Promise me you'll try it, Lane. It'll work out fine."

Lane was looking past his shoulder as she nodded. "Looks like someone else is waiting to see you, captain."

The officer turned his head to see Steve Bard and Jim Blade sitting their horses a few yards away, waiting. It was apparent they had just ridden in, for the sentry was closing the gate through which they had just entered the fort. Jackson turned his gaze back to the woman, frowning at the obvious interruption.

"Think it over, Lane. We'll talk some more about it."

Lane hesitated, then nodded. She turned and walked toward the encampment, but her head was held a little higher, her back a bit straighter than when she had come out of the sutler's store moments earlier.

The two horsemen urged their horses forward until they were close to the captain. He jerked his head toward his office.

"Learn anything?" the officer asked, keeping his voice low. He had voiced the thought to no one, but after the exposure of Kalispell Kane as an outlaw and a possible spy, he didn't know whom he could trust.

"Nothin' real special, captain," Bard replied, but there was a worried shake of his head. "Just some strange goings on near the reservation boundary."

"We'd better talk in my office," Jackson announced, as he cast a glance toward Lane Lester's retreating back. He didn't understand her anger. Maybe she didn't either.

Moments later, the captain was seated behind his desk, while the scout and the journalist stood in front of him.

"The big guy that held his gun on us tried to pass off all the gunfire as a wolf hunt," Bard was explaining, "but somethin' else had to be going on."

As Bard made his report, Blade glanced about, saw a chair against the wall and backed up to slump into it. His expression plainly stated that he was not military, he did not have to stand at attention for anyone. Not any more.

"And the man that stopped us took king-size measures to see that we didn't really find out what was going on," Blade offered from his seat.

"What did the man look like?" the captain wanted to know, glancing at Blade, then returning his gaze to Bard's face.

"I think I seen him here in the fort last night," Bard stated, then went on to offer a physical description of the man who had stopped them. At the end he added, "And he's wearin' two six-guns. Acts like he knows how to use them."

The captain nodded. "Sounds like Jack Gentleman. He's foreman of Jud Ransom's rancho."

Blade suddenly rose from his chair. "Not aiming to change the subject, captain, but who was that beautiful girl you were talking with when we rode in?"

Jackson could not help but show his annoyance at having his thoughts interrupted. "Lane Lester. She came out here with her brother to build a saloon in Silver Hill, but he died. She was still in the mining camp until the Indian troubles started. She came here with the others for protection."

In spite of the officer's terse words, Blade offered a grin, pretending to smother a yawn. "I'd better let the pair of you discuss the Indian problem and the wolves. I feel the need for some air."

Both men watched as Blade stalked to the door and closed it behind him. Then the scowling captain turned his attention back to Bard. He nodded toward the door.

"What's the story on him? What's he doing here?"

"Might do to ask him yourself, captain." There was a note of coolness in the scout's tone, which Jackson ignored.

"You seem to be his buddy. I'm asking you."

Bard hesitated for a moment, then offered a shrug. "He says he's a journalist. Writes stories about the west for *Harper's Weekly*, some others."

The officer's eyes narrowed. "He's going to write about us? About Fort Wingate?"

That brought another shrug. "I don't know what he's goin' to write, captain. We're not good enough buddies that we talk that much."

Captain Jackson lowered his head, thinking for a moment, then looked up, an expression of resignation in his eyes. "I could order him out of the fort, but that would only be adding fuel to whatever fire he has burning." He hesitated for a moment before adding, "If he's writing for *Harper's Weekly*, it ought to be more truthful than the trash that Ned Buntline is writing about Bill Cody and Wild Bill Hickok."

"I'd think so, captain," Bard agreed. He was aware that the officer was thinking of his own career. He didn't want to be stuck in frontier posts until he turned gray. If he did a good job at the fort while the colonel was away it might help his future. If things went wrong, his chances of promotion and transfer would die.

"Do you really think there was anything serious connected with what you experienced this morning? Anything to do with our problems here?" The captain was still scowling in spite of the change of subject. It all dealt with his military future.

All Bard could do was offer a shrug. "It just seemed mighty strange the way it happened, captain."

Lane Lester had her laundry bundled in a sheet as she crossed the street and gained the board sidewalk that fronted the structures. She was frowning as she walked, thinking about her conversation with the fort's captain.

"Lane!"

The voice was low but harsh. Lane Lester turned to see Jack Gentleman step from between two buildings. The woman offered him one of her pent-up glares, but Gentleman ignored it, smiling.

"I've a need to talk to you."

"What about?"

"Us. Why've you been avoiding me?"

Lane's tone was one of distaste as she stated, "I've always avoided you."

The smile began to fade on the gunman's face. "You were

always happy enough to see me when you and your brother was workin' that saloon back in Dodge City."

"That was business. You came there to drink and gamble. We were in business to supply your wants and take your money."

Gentleman stepped closer, suddenly grabbing her arm. The smile was gone, his lips being compressed into a tight straight line. Lane, grimacing at the tightness of the gunman's hold, attempted to twist away, dropping her laundry bundle in her struggles. Gentleman tightened his grip on her arm even more.

"I used to think you liked me," he gritted.

"Let me go!" Lane demanded, her voice reflecting the pain she was feeling from the tight grip.

"Who is it?" the gunman demanded. "That blue-belly captain?"

Lane offered no reply. She was close to tears as she struggled against Gentleman's vise-like grip.

"She asked nice. Let her go, mister," a voice said behind them.

Chapter Ten

Jim Blade had just come out of the sutler's store, a supply of fresh cigars stuffed in his jacket pocket. As he eyed Jack Gentleman, his face wore a smile that was so amiable that it could only be interpreted as dangerous.

Gentleman whirled, swinging Lane about by the wrist he still gripped. She uttered a stifled scream at the pain created by the twisting movement. Her captor seemed not to notice. Gentleman's full attention was on Blade, who took a few steps toward the pair. With a jerk, Lane Lester was able to break free. Gentleman didn't even glance at her as she stepped away. His eyes were on Blade and both hands were creeping toward the butts of the matching six-guns hanging from his belt.

Lane Lester's first thought was to run for the encampment to get away from the pair facing each other, but she couldn't. Standing in the middle of the street, she looked from one man to the other. It was difficult to determine whether she was entranced by the drama taking place before her or was simply in a state of shock at the rough treatment from the gunman.

"You followed along to be certain Bard and I could find our way back here to the fort?" the journalist asked quietly, raising an eyebrow to tell the other man he didn't believe it.

"You're mixin' in my business, Blade," Gentleman warned, his expression verging on a snarl.

Blade's smile remained on his lips, but it was suddenly less amiable. He halted, facing Gentleman. "Apparently you know who I am. If you touch that gun I'll kill you."

There was no threat in the words; it came across as a simple statement of fact. The offhand declaration surprised Gentleman. His hands hovered over his six-guns indecisively. He had seen Blade shoot Kalispell Kane. He knew the smiling man could handle a gun. After a moment, his hands dropped and he forced a smile that expressed more than a trace of arrogance. He shook his head.

"This is no place for a gunfight," he announced. After a moment, he added, "But we'll be meetin' again."

Blade offered an agreeable nod. "Any time, Jack. I've always been the obliging type."

Gentleman turned to stalk away between the two buildings from where he had come. Blade watched him for a moment, then turned to step to Lane Lester's side. The crisis ended, she was gathering up the laundry that had been dropped during the melee. The journalist offered her his arm.

"I'd appreciate the pleasure of your company, miss, wherever it is you're going."

Her laundry wrapped in a sheet and held under one arm, Lane hesitated for a moment, then offered a grave nod and took his arm. Together, they sauntered toward the encampment.

Two army wives stood in the door of the sutler's store. They had watched most of the face-off, strangely intrigued by the harsh drama that had taken place. One of the women, well-dressed and wearing a bonnet, offered an indignant toss of her head.

"Imagine! A hussy like that allowing men to fight over her right here in the fort!"

The other woman, gray-haired and dowdy, shook her head in disgust. "I don't know why Captain Jackson allows her to stay here. He ought to send her packing!"

Neither Lane nor Blade heard the exchange as they neared the boundaries of the refugee encampment. At a space between two wagons that served as an entry to the inhabited arena, Lane paused. Blade stopped, too, knowing this was as far as he was supposed to go.

"I don't know how well you know Jack Gentleman," the woman stated, "but you'll have to watch out for him from now on. He's a killer."

Blade offered an agreeable nod. "I'll keep that in mind." There was a moment's hesitation before he asked, "How'd you get tangled up with a man like that?"

"It was in Dodge City. My brother owned the gambling franchise in a saloon and I worked there with him. Jack Gentleman was one of our customers."

She paused, eyeing the hard-packed dirt street where Gentleman was riding toward the fort's entrance. The sentry already was swinging open the heavy gate for the rider's exit. The gunman looked neither left nor right, but Lane Lester was certain he had been watching them both as he rode past. She turned back to Jim Blade.

"He killed a drunk buffalo skinner in a gunfight on Front Street," the woman explained. "A couple of the skinner's brothers swore they'd get him, but they both got shot in the back."

"And nothing was ever proved that he did it," Blade offered, nodding his understanding of frontier law—or the lack of it.

"I don't suppose you approve of saloon women." Coming from Lane Lester, it was a statement of fact rather than a question. It caused Blade to grin and shake his head.

"Why shouldn't I? That's where my father met my mother!"

The woman stared at him in disbelief for a moment, then burst out laughing. He laughed with her.

"You're a friend of that Indian scout," she observed. "What does he think of saloon women?"

That brought an amused shake of Blade's head. "Steve Bard? I don't think he believes they're here to stay."

"Saloon women?" Lane was puzzled, perhaps a bit disappointed at his comment. It showed and Blade chuckled at her expression.

"No. Just women in general. I'm not even certain he knows they're different from men!"

Blade had expected her to laugh at his joke, but she only nodded, offering a little frown.

"Thanks for helping me, Mr. Blade. It certainly wasn't a situation of my choosing."

"My pleasure, ma'am, but call me Jim. I'm always ready, willing and able to aid a lady in distress. Besides, I don't like Gentleman." He shook his head, watching the fort's gate swing shut behind the rider. "His name certainly doesn't fit his personality."

Lane edged toward the opening between the wagons. "I have to get some things done, Jim, but thanks, again."

As she turned to make her way across a wagon tongue without tripping, Blade looked after her. He was wondering whether Steve Bard had any idea that Lane Lester was interested in him.

He also wondered how she had managed to remain a lady in Dodge City. He had been there several years earlier, when it had been called Buffalo City. Even then it was a tough town with few decent women about. When the Atchison, Topeka and Santa Fe Railroad had extended its tracks through the town, it had been renamed Dodge City after a nearby military outpost, Fort Dodge.

The railroad had brought the buffalo hunters and skinners to the town, carting fortunes in buffalo hides that were stacked six feet high along the railroad, waiting to be hauled to markets in the east.

In Dodge City during the buffalo-shipping era, bison skinners came to be called "stinkers," because of the smell of rotting meat that seemed to permeate their very bodies as well as their clothing.

There were two Front Streets in Dodge City, one on each side of the railroad. The area on the north side was made up of shops and residences; no guns were allowed there. The south side was peopled by the buffalo hunters, skinners, gamblers and drifters, who hung out in the saloons and houses of ill repute. The town's permanent population was a little over 1,000, with nineteen concerns in the liquor business.

Jim Blade was aware that the buffalo were nearly gone, but Dodge City's health as a community had been bolstered by the herds made up of thousands of cattle coming out of Texas that were loaded into stock cars from the railroad's shipping pens.

Blade shook his head. Lane Lester could consider herself lucky that she had a brother to look out for her in those wild surroundings. He glanced around the fort, wondering how she was going to manage on her own.

The journalist also wondered about Jack Gentleman. Blade had been called upon several times to defend himself with his own six-gun, but more often had been able to bluff his way out of tight situations. He had been successful this time with Gentleman, but he couldn't ignore Lane Lester's statement that some of the gunman's enemies had ended with bullets in their backs.

With a sigh, Blade turned to look in the direction of the fort commander's office, wondering how much longer Steve Bard was going to be tied up with the captain.

Chapter Eleven

Jud Ransom was standing beside his corral fence, watching one of his men attempt to ride a young paint horse that had been captured and added to the ranch remuda. The rider had been thrown twice and was less than enthusiastic about another try.

"Get up in that saddle and try to keep his head up!" Ransom shouted at the rider. The man cast him a baleful look, then shook his head.

"Not me, boss. I signed on to take my chances at bein' shot, not to get killed by some crazy cayuse!"

"You was hired to do what I tell you!" Ransom snarled. Two other men were in the corral, holding the horse, one of them twisting an ear to maintain the animal's attention. Both of them glanced at the rider, then at Ransom. Their expressions suggested it would be interesting to see where this confrontation went.

Frank and Jesse James, as well as their two followers, were leaning on the top rail on the opposite side of the corral from where Ransom was positioned. All four had been watching the battle with the young stallion, but now they found the situation between the would-be rough stock rider and the ranch owner of even greater interest.

"Better turn the horse loose, Mr. Ransom." Jack Gentleman called as he strode toward the corral. Ransom, scowling, turned to glare at him. Gentleman gestured to the flatlands below the ranch headquarters.

"Injuns comin'," he announced. "Looks like Long Arm and some of his braves. Looks like th' kid what was guardin' them steers is with them!"

Ransom turned to look across the corral. "Get th' saddle off that horse and turn him loose. Then you all get to th' bunkhouse and stay there!" He turned to wave an arm at the four train robbers on the other side of the corral.

"You all get out of sight, too. I don't want that kid to maybe recognize you!"

From where they stood, the James gang could not see the plain below, but the three men in the corral had turned to look down the hill to where the Indians were approaching, their horses at a trot, a quarter mile away. It only took the trio seconds to strip the hackamore off the horse's head after loosening the saddle cinch and stripping the leather off the horse's back. The horse snorted and whirled, aiming a kick at the closest man, who managed to duck.

The three headed for the corral gate, one of them lugging the saddle, another carrying the hackamore. Gentleman had drifted to the gate to open it so they could rush through it. Meantime, Jesse and the others had started to circle the corral, moving toward the low adobe building that housed the ranch's riders.

"You'd best get out of sight too, Jack," Ransom stated, glancing at his foreman. "Long Arm don't like you much."

"That feeling's somewhat mutual," the gun hawk muttered in reply, but he turned to follow the others.

Ransom pretended not to see the approaching band of

half a dozen Navajos. Standing with his back toward them, he appeared to be concentrating on the paint horse that now trotted around the corral. As Ransom watched, the horse suddenly stopped, staring in the direction of the Indians, who were less than fifty yards away. The animal arched his neck, lifted its head and uttered a high-pitched whinny that was almost a scream. It was obvious one or more of the Navajos also rode stallions. The sound issuing from the paint stallion was that of a challenge.

Ransom lazily turned to look toward the approaching Navajos, then stepped away from the corral fence. He raised his right hand, open palm outward, in the sign of peace, holding it aloft until Long Arm matched the gesture. The Indian said something to his men and they drew up their mounts, sitting them in a loose formation, as Long Arm rode forward to face the renegade rancher.

"I wasn't expectin' you, Long Arm." Ransom glanced past him to the other Indians. None of them looked particularly warlike at the moment, although several had rifles balanced across the withers of their horses. "What brings this visit?"

Long Arm had received a smattering of education in a reservation school and spoke a gutteral sort of English to which one had to listen closely in order to understand. As a result of continued dealings with the Navajo, Ransom had become reasonably proficient in understanding what was said. The Indian waved an arm in the direction of the other horsemen.

"My people. They say how long 'fore we burn fort, kill soldiers. Take guns!" Anger twisted the Indian's features and he tended to spit out the words. "Soldiers steal our cattle. We want cattle. Guns, too!"

Ransom took a cigar from his vest pocket and extended it toward Long Arm. The Indian waved it away, gaze centered on the white man's face. Ransom bit the end off the cigar and searched his pocket for matches, as he spoke.

"That's the cattle I sold th' army so they could pass them on to you and your people? Your regular quarterly rations, right?" Ransom pretended he was having trouble understanding the situation. He found a match and scratched it on a corral rail, holding it to his cigar as Long Arm heeled his horse a step closer and bent to stare into Ransom's face.

"My people say attack fort. Now!"

Although the Navajo's demeanor was one of threat, Ransom calmly puffed at the cigar and turned his head to blow out the smoke. He was careful not to blow it in Long Arm's face. He turned back to look at the Indian, nodding.

"Long Arm, I want the soldiers driven out just as much as you do. Maybe even more." He waved a hand loosely in the direction of the other Indians who were watching. "But you only have a handful of warriors who've fled the reservation. You don't have enough people to take on the United States Cavalry!"

Ransom was aware the fort was undermanned and that its troops of cavalry spent most of their time patrolling the area between the settlements and the boundaries of the Navajo Reservation, which had been established in 1868. Fort Defiance, abandoned by the military, was now the reservation's headquarters. It was less than forty miles away.

Ransom also realized that there still were too many soldiers for a direct attack on Fort Wingate. He felt that if such an attack came, the thin ranks of the cavalry troops would be backed by the men in the settlers' camp. He was certain Long Arm also was aware of this likelihood, but the angry Indian was growing less cautious day by day.

"About those cattle," Ransom said, taking another puff on

the stogie. "Have you tried to track them? See where they were taken?"

"Soldiers drove cows into river," the Indian declared. "Cattle out other side few at a time, different places." The Navajo shook his head, scowling. "Tracks all mixed now with your cattle."

Ransom seemed to think about it for a moment, staring at the ash on his cigar, then looking up at the mounted redskin.

"They probably drove them through my herd and bunched them up somewhere on the other side. Sounds like an Apache trick to me."

Long Arm shook his head. "No! Soldiers! All horses have iron shoes. No Apaches!" He turned to point to one of the young warriors behind him. "He see! Soldiers! They shoot at him! Try to kill! Steal cattle! My people go hungry!"

Ransom held up a hand to placate the renegade Navajo. "Hold up a minute. I sold th' Army fifty steers for your people. That's what you got?"

Long Arm jerked a nod. "Fifty. Then they steal fifty!"

Ransom waved toward the band of Indians. "Tell you what. You have your people cut fifty steers out of my herd. Drive them down to your reservation. Feed your people." He hesitated for a moment allowing the offer to sink in.

"Soldiers maybe steal, again!"

He could send back the same steers that the James gang had stolen from the Indians. If the Navajo braves were hungry, their children going without food, they might be more willing to fight the blue coats. On the other hand, his seeming to care for the Indians' plight should pay off in the end.

"How many warriors do you have now? Men who will follow you against the blue coats?"

Long Arm held up one hand to display five fingers, then opened and closed it several times. Ransom was making rapid calculations. The show of fingers added up to about forty-five. He shook his head.

"Not enough men, chief." Long Arm was not a chief. He was simply a reservation jumper who had taken some other dissidents with him. Ransom was aware of this, but it didn't hurt to stroke the redskin's ego.

"Other men leave reservation now. Some come to Massacre Mountain each night, where we hide. Soon we have many."

"Two times as many as now?"

The question brought a nod from the scowling Indian. "More. Many more!"

Ransom dropped his half-smoked cigar in the dust and ground out the smoldering ash with his boot heel before looking up at Long Arm, nodding.

"The time will soon be right, Long Arm. A few more days. Then we'll punish the soldiers who steal food from your children."

"How many days?" the Indian demanded.

"A week. Maybe less."

"Seven days? Then we attack?"

"Sooner maybe. I'll send someone to determine where the soldiers are weakest. What would be the best way to attack them. Then I'll tell you when." That had been the job he had assigned to Kalispell Kane, but the damned fool had gotten himself killed before he had come up with any useful information. No need for Long Arm to know that, though.

"My warriors be ready. We take cattle now!" He raised his hand once more and flicked it closed and shut ten times. Ransom nodded.

"That's right. Fifty head."

As the Indians rode away, Ransom stood watching for a few moments, then turned and strode up the hill to his house a hundred yards away. He had just smoked his last cigar and wanted to get more to fill out his coat pocket.

In the house, he opened the humidor on his desk and extracted several of the crudely wrapped stogies that he ordered periodically from New Orleans. No telling where they came from originally, but he enjoyed them, so origin and maker didn't matter.

As he was aligning the cigars in his breast pocket, there was a rap on the door and he paused to look in that direction.

"Come in!" he called, expecting it to be Jack Gentleman. Instead, it was Jesse James who was framed in the doorway. Brother Frank was at his shoulder.

"What'd the Indians want, Jud?" Jesse asked mildly, as he and Frank stepped into the room to face the one-time guerrilla.

"Long Arm and his braves are gettin' restless. They're mad 'bout th' blue bellies stealin' their cattle. They wanta kill someone!" He could not suppress a twisted grin.

"Are you runnin' things or is the Indian?" Jesse James wanted to know.

"Takin' those steers must've turned his whole tribe against the Fort Wingate people. They're ready to fight." Ransom hesitated for a moment to stare at the two Missouri outlaws. "I'll need you and your men to help with the attack. Maybe work from inside the fort."

"What do you have in mind for us?" Frank James wanted to know.

"Gentleman says you seemed to get along okay with that Indian scout. If you was staked out inside the fort, you could maybe overpower the sentry on that gate and open it for the Injuns and the rest of my men."

"Sounds like a real slaughter," Jesse observed. "Almost as bad as that mess back in Kansas. Not just soldiers. Men, women and children in the camp. Civilians."

"Like the Lawrence raid." Ransom nodded in acknowledgement. "I want you and your men ready for it."

"We're ready now, except for one thing," Jesse James announced quietly, eyes on the rancher's face.

"What's that? What do you mean?"

Jesse James mouth suddenly twisted in a show of distaste. It was as though he had eaten something that didn't agree with him.

"We're not doing it, Jud. We ain't ridin' with you." The edict was spoken quietly.

Ransom glared at the two train robbers, eyes suddenly narrowing. "I'm countin' on you! I need you inside that fort, dammit!"

"Me and Frank didn't shoot women and children in Lawrence and we ain't startin' now. We're more at home in a nice, clean bank or chasin' down a money train!"

"Besides, we have our own chores ahead of us," Frank James put in. "Summer's comin' on and we have to be in California to make our search for Pa's grave. We promised our Ma!"

"You owe me!" Ransom snarled at the pair, looking from one to the other. "I've hidden you from the Texas Ranger that's after you."

Jesse shook his head. "There ain't no Ranger after us or we'd know about it. As for th' few days of bunk and board you've furnished, stealin' them cattle from that Indian pays any debt we might have. All four of us are gone from here tonight!"

The door to Ransom's office had been left open when the pair of outlaws had entered. Jack Gentleman suddenly was framed there, a six-gun in each of his hands.

"Trouble, Jud?" he asked quietly.

Chapter Twelve

Jesse James, eyes cold and deadly, was staring at Ransom's gun hawk. His hands were at his sides, seemingly relaxed and nowhere near the gun that hung from his old cavalry holster.

"You might get me," Jesse declared, tone heavy with quiet menace, "but Frank's certain to kill you. It works the other way around, too. No matter who you choose, one of us'll kill you."

In reply to the threat, Jack Gentleman thumbed back the hammers on his matched six-guns. Behind his desk, Ransom raised a hand to halt any action the gunman might take.

"He's right, Jack. Pull a trigger and you're a dead! Put away those guns!"

Gentleman cast the rancher a look of surprise, hesitating for an instant before he lowered the muzzles of the two revolvers. He carefully lowered the hammers before holstering the blue-steel weapons. As this was happening, the James brothers seemed to ignore him and turned their attention back to Ransom.

"Like we said, thanks for everything, Jud, but we're ridin' out," Jesse told him. Ransom was frowning as he offered a shrug that was meant to signify acceptance.

"Guess I can't have everything my own way all the time. I wish you luck in California."

Jesse simply nodded and turned toward the door, while Frank hesitated for a moment, eyeing Ransom.

"Thanks, again, Jud." He was a little less angry than Jesse, but turned to follow his brother. Gentleman, scowling, was blocking the door.

"Get out of their way, Jack." Ransom's quiet words were an order. "They're off to California."

Gentleman sidled away from the doorway, watching as the pair passed into the darkness of an adjoining room and closed the door behind them. When he turned to face the man on the other side of the desk, his eyes were narrowed and there was an expression of disgust, maybe even contempt on his face.

"No guts, huh?" He was referring to his employer, but Ransom took the other's words wrong.

"They have guts. And they're dangerous." It was his turn to frown as he settled back in his chair. "They know more about what's going on than is safe for us."

"I can take some men. Ride out and gun them down."

Ransom shook his head. "I need you here."

"You could have Long Arm and his braves take care of them. Might let him know they was the soldiers that stole the cattle."

Ransom offered another negative shake of his head as he ran his hand through his hair, rumpling it.

"I don't want them slaughtered on our own doorstep. Wish I knew just where they're headed for in California."

"I heard Clell Miller talkin' in th' bunkhouse. The James boys think their old man's buried up around Marysville somewhere."

"Any idea where Marysville might be?" Ransom asked. "I never heard of it."

"It's in the gold country somewheres north of Sacramento from what I heard them say."

Ransom considered this information for a moment, then eyed Gentleman with a hint of amusement on his lips.

"We could let the good citizens of Marysville take care of them," he said slowly, voicing his thoughts. "Let them do our bushwhacking for us."

He arose and circled the desk to face his foreman. "Get one of the boys to ride to Santa Fe. I'll write out the message and we'll have him telegraph Marysville. Let the law there know who's comin' to visit."

Gentleman grinned, as he nodded. "I'll go myself. I could use a couple of days in Santa Fe."

Ransom shook his head. "I need you here. You're a familiar sight at the fort. Accepted. I want you and a couple of your boys to sort of alternate hangin' out there. Get a handle on what's going on. Try to find out what kind of weapons them settlers have got."

Gentleman's grin had disappeared and he offered a sigh of resignation. At least he'd have a reason for being at Fort Wingate. He might get another chance at Lane Lester. Or he might even find a chance to gun down that wise ass, who had crossed him. "I'll saddle up now," Gentleman announced. "I should be able to get there before dark maybe."

From the fort's drill hall came the sound of a fiddle being tuned as several couples that included two junior officers and their ladies walked down the street to where a huge, hand-painted sign was erected. It read:

PUBLIC DANCE TONIGHT
COME ONE! COME ALL!
MUSIC UNTIL DAWN!

The drill hall was a long, low structure fashioned from hand-hewn lumber. At the far end of the hall a low stage had been erected and a four-piece band was tuning up. Two of the musicians—the trumpeter and a piano player—were soldiers in their working uniform. A man well past middle age with a beard that was more white than gray was wearing clean but worn canvas pants, an out-of-fashion coat and playing his fiddle, while a younger settler similarly clad strummed a guitar.

At the other end of the room, several women from the settlers' camp were hovering over a large punch bowl. Captain Jackson had talked—possibly threatened—Simon Westphal into supplying the liquors needed to give the punch character. Bobbing about in the mixture was evidence of dried peaches and plums that had been volunteered by some of the settlers.

On the worn ponderosa surface that was to serve as a dance floor, perhaps a dozen couples were waiting for the music to begin. Several soldiers, officer and enlisted, were among them. All wore the working clothes of the cavalry rather than the resplendent formal Army garb normally worn for such occasions. Wooden straight-backed chairs were lined up against one wall and some of them were occupied by soldiers and settlers.

Captain Jackson had been loitering on the sidelines, watching the musicians as they tuned their instruments. Finally, the man with the beard looked at the officer and offered a quick nod.

Jackson strode across the floor to stand in front of the quartet of musicians, facing the gathering. The trumpeter blew a meaningless blast on his horn and the conversation quickly died, as all present turned to look at the officer. There was total quiet as he began to speak.

"As some of you know, one of your own, Miss Lane Lester has gone to a good deal of trouble to plan a good time for all of us." He paused waiting and the hint was taken. There was some polite applause. Lane Lester, standing against the wall near the punch bowl, looked surprised at the unexpected mention by the fort commander. She was dressed in a laundered and ironed dress of cotton that was somewhat tight across her bosom. However, the collar was high and buttoned almost to her chin.

"The sign outside says Music Until Dawn. I just want to say that anyone who leaves here before the sun comes up will be ordered to appear in front of me before noon to face charges having to do with dereliction of duty!" He was smiling as he made the threat and there was general laughter. The applause for his short speech was more pronounced than had been for Lane Lester.

"Ladies and gentlemen, you've been living out there on our parade ground in other than ideal circumstances. I'm sorry I can't offer you anything better, but this is still the frontier. I only hope you enjoy yourselves tonight, one and all!"

He turned to motion to the bearded man, apparently the leader of the band as well as the fiddler. A lively tune was struck up and those on the dance floor began to follow it. Others came off the sidelines to join the dancing. The captain edged along the dance floor until he was facing Lane. He offered a semi-bow, grinning at her.

"I think this'll make folks feel a bit better, thanks to you. Might I have this dance, Miss Lester?"

Surprising herself, the woman found herself smiling as she nodded. "I'd be delighted, sir." Others were watching as the captain and the lady gambler began to glide among the others.

"Your party seems to be a great success," Jackson murmured in her ear as he looked about. Lane wore a quizzical expression as she looked at his face.

"You didn't order your soldiers to be here tonight, did you?" She had observed that virtually ever soldier on the post was present, except for those charged with the fort's guard duty.

"What would ever give you that idea?" Jackson asked, doing his best to look totally innocent.

Lane, though, was looking over his shoulder. She had not seen Jim Blade come in, but he was leaning against the wall near the door. Other than the captain, she felt he may have been the best dressed man in the room or maybe it was simply because he was the cleanest.

He wore a white shirt with a black string tie. His boots were polished and his trousers appeared to have been sponged and pressed, probably by one of the enlisted wives who did laundry for the soldiers. Blade wore a new double-breasted jacket that she knew had come from Simon Westphal's stock. She had seen it on display in the sutler's store. Westphal kept a small supply of civilian clothing for those who might be discharged, transferred to another post or going on leave and did not want to travel in uniform.

Blade saw Lane looking at him and offered a wink. She considered returning the wink, then thought better of it. She was attempting to cultivate an image as a lady. A gambler, yes, but at least a lady gambler.

As she was whirled away by the captain, Lane saw the door open to allow Steve Bard to enter. He looked tired and disheveled, wearing his buckskin shirt, his hat on the back of his head. He glanced about and removed the hat as Blade frowned at him. Lane wished she could hear the exchange between the two, but the captain was moving her away, gliding between the other couples.

Blade glanced at Bard, looking him up and down, not particularly impressed with his Indian scout attire. "Where've you been?"

"Looking around the fort." Bard's eyes were surveying the gathering. He seemed to be counting the number of soldiers present. Two of the fort's troops were somewhere to the north near the Navajo reservation, patrolling the boundaries for departing Indians. There were less than forty soldiers in the fort at the moment. Most of them were there in the drill hall.

"Don't you ever relax?" Blade wanted to know. The music had ended and a number of the dancers were headed for the punch bowl and the assorted finger sandwiches that awaited consumption. Lane had made the sandwiches herself, scrounging some ingredients from the military mess hall, plus using what delicacies she could find in Simon Westphal's store, telling him Captain Jackson would pay for them.

As the musicians took a breather, the captain was in conversation with one of the settlers, an elderly man who considered himself spokesman for the encampment. Lane Lester edged along the dance floor, but hesitated as she saw the door open, admitting Jack Gentleman, who was dressed as he always was, including his twin six-guns. Lane ignored the gunman, pausing in front of Steve Bard. She forced a smile.

"Care to dance, Mr. Bard?"

Bard did not attempt to match her smile. He shook his head, thoughts plainly centered on more serious business. "Sorry, ma'am. Not t'night."

Lane Lester's smile faded as she kept her eyes on Bard's features. He was looking past her, still counting soldiers.

"Your manners aren't nearly as polished as the seat of your pants, mister," she ground at him. It was enough to at least draw his gaze to her angry frown. He shook his head stubbornly.

"Sorry, miss. I have to see the captain on a matter."

Jackson was headed toward them, smiling at Lane as he approached. Bard stepped in front of the woman to cut off the officer.

"Captain, I need to talk to you."

Jackson glanced uneasily from Bard to Lane, then back again. In the background, Jack Gentleman was watching the exchange. Bard jerked his head toward the door.

"Outside?" the captain wanted to know, puzzled and perhaps a bit worried. Bard nodded and turned to lead the way out into the darkness. Lane Lester stared after the pair, her anger at being ignored suddenly apparent. Jim Blade glanced at her as the musicians began to work over another tune.

"May I have the next dance, Miss Lester?" Blade asked. The girl turned to him, doing her best to adopt a smile.

"I wondered when you were going to ask me."

Putting an arm around the woman's waist, Jim Blade moved her onto the dance floor. Jack Gentleman leaned against the wall, thumbs tucked in his gun belt, watching the pair with a scowl.

The fort's aging sergeant major had spotted Gentleman and marched up to him. "Mr. Gentleman, this is a social event. We allow no firearms here tonight. You'll have to shed them or leave."

Gentleman dropped his gaze from the dance floor to offer the aging soldier a sneer.

"I'm not one of your soldier boys, Sergeant Blue Belly. I do what I want!"

Chapter Thirteen

Sergeant Major Seth Keene was a veteran of more than thirty years military service. Most of that time had been spent in dealing with people, good and bad. Jack Gentleman started to push past Keene, but the elderly soldier side-stepped to stay in front of him, continuing to block his path.

"Your guns are not welcome here, Mr. Gentleman." The sergeant major's tone was severe but formal. "Leave immediately or I'll have you arrested and thrown in our guardhouse. Then Captain Jackson and your Mr. Ransom can work out what's to be done about you!"

Gentleman still was scowling, but nodded agreement and took a step to the rear. He slowly unbuckled his gun belt and handed it to the sergeant major with a twisted grin. "Take good care of them, Blue Belly. They're my livelihood."

Seth Keene held the gun rig as he might a dead skunk and deposited it on the seat of a chair beside the door. In spite of the way he had stood up to Gentleman, he was worried. He knew a man of violence when he saw one. As the gun hawk eyed Lane Lester dancing with Jim Blade, the sergeant major turned to look out the open doorway to where his cap-

92

tain and Steve Bard were standing in the street. He could not hear what was being said, but it was obvious that Captain Jackson was somewhat angry. Bard was on the receiving end of that anger, as he eyed the cavalry officer.

"I don't know where you learned your manners, Mr. Bard, but you did not have to be quite so disagreeable with that young lady."

Bard's tone carried ice and his eyes were hard as he replied. "Did you have to throw a party when the Indians are ready to burn down your gates?"

"What do you mean? You knew about the dance!"

"I didn't know that you were going to cut the sentries on duty so they could trip the light fantastic. Where did you learn soldiering?" Bard's words were spoken in a slow cadence meant to underline the importance of what he was saying. Jackson stiffened at the tone and what had been said.

"Running this fort as I see fit is my responsibility."

"I saw Jack Gentleman's here. Doesn't he have a reputation as a gunman and a troublemaker?"

The officer was becoming perturbed at the Indian scout's attitude. It was visible in the stern features he was displaying. "As long as he behaves himself, I have no legal reason to ban him from the fort."

Less than ten yards away, inside the drill hall, Gentleman was staring toward the dancing couples with eyes smoldering, especially one couple in particular. As the music ended, Jim Blade and Lane Lester were close enough that the gunman could hear their conversation.

"It's warm in here," Blade stated, looking down at her. He was nearly a foot taller. "Could I get you a glass of that punch?"

Lane nodded as she found a seat against the wall and slid onto it. "That would be nice. If you would, please." Lane looked after him as he worked his way through the crowd, trying to reach the punch bowl. A smile touched her lips, as the musicians began to play once more and couples edged onto the floor.

"Care to dance, ma'am?" It was Jack Gentleman standing beside her. He bent from the waist and extended his hand as though to help her to her feet. The woman shook her head, scowling at him.

"No! Not with you!"

Gentleman's smile was somewhat wolfish although he was attempting to appear gallant. "That's no way to treat a guest in a nice, friendly gathering, ma'am."

Lane rose abruptly and started to turn away, but Gentleman grabbed her wrist, clamping down with hard fingers. The smile was gone as he pushed his face close to her, growling in a low tone.

"You wouldn't want a scene here in front of all these nice folks. Come on outside where I can talk to you."

Lane considered screaming for help, but Gentleman had been correct in his evaluation. She did not want to create a scene that would reflect badly upon her. She already had enough problems in that regard. Gentleman maintained his grip on the woman's wrist, levering her toward the open doorway. Captain Jackson and Steve Bard, standing in the street, did not see the two come out of the hall. They were too engrossed in their own discussion.

"Mr. Bard, I've listened to your complaints and what I take to be your advice, but until the colonel returns from Washington, I'll run this command as I see fit. You can put me on report with him then, if you like."

Steve Bard, face heavy with anger and disgust, started to reply, but the captain cut him off. "You are not an officer. For all practical purposes, you are an investigator. For the present, I'll thank you to mind your own business. Is that understood?"

In spite of his expression, Bard's tone was calm as he replied. "Yes, sir. Perfectly."

His piece said, Jackson's attitude softened a trifle, as he nodded toward the drill hall and the music issuing from it.

"It's a party, Steve. Go enjoy yourself." He half turned to look in the direction of the fort headquarters. "I have to get something out of my office."

Jackson whirled and stalked off into the darkness as Bard stared after him, slowly shaking his head. He had dealt with many officers in two armies—Confederate and Union—over his years. When a young one was saddled with such responsibility as running a fort even on a temporary basis, that individual invariably felt he had to live up to a command image. As he mused, the Indian scout took a cigar out of a pocket and started to light it.

"Why can't you just leave me alone, Jack?"

Lane Lester's voice was low, but troubled enough for Bard to turn his head toward the narrow veranda that fronted the drill hall. The light coming out the open door of the hall enabled him to see that Lane Lester was backed against the structure's wall and Jack Gentleman was hulking over her. Bard dropped his cigar, hesitating for a moment.

"Look at yourself, Lane. No one here has much use for you. You'd best remember who your friends are." Gentleman's voice was gutteral with raw emotion.

"You're no friend. You're nothing but a killer!" the woman's voice was louder, almost as though she was seeking help. Gentleman suddenly bent forward, clamping his lips to hers, holding her close despite her struggles. The voice behind the pair was soft, almost conversational.

"Try to live up to your name, Gentleman. Leave the lady be."

The suggestion caused Gentleman to jerk away from Lane Lester, whirling to face Steve Bard, who now stood in the street below the steps to the veranda. The two men stared at each other for a long moment, while Lane leaned against the wall, wiping her lips with her fist, trying not to allow tears. After a long moment, Gentleman forced himself to relax, forcing a sardonic smile.

"You ought to stick to scoutin', mister."

Bard returned Gentleman's smile, his tone still conversational. "If someone told the folks inside you've been forcin' yourself on a lady, you'd most likely get lynched. I'd hate to see that."

Bard had noted that Gentleman was not wearing his matching six-guns. His own Single Action Army Colt was lying on the bunk he had been assigned in one of the enlisted barracks. He assumed that Gentleman also had noted that neither of them was armed.

Gentleman continued to stare at Bard for a moment, still smiling in his arrogant fashion. He glanced at Lane, who stood with her back pressed to the wall, watching the two of them, as she dabbed at her tears. Gentleman offered a shrug and started down the steps as though to pass Bard. Only a pace away, he suddenly charged the scout, swinging a fist to the man's chin. Bard, caught by surprise, staggered backward, almost falling.

Gentleman had expected his punch to flatten the scout in the dust of the street. Instead, Bard managed to recover his balance and moved in, alternating his punches with both fists. A blow to the stomach of the gunman doubled him over. A rabbit punch behind his ear was enough to make Gentleman whirl away, trying to recover from the blow's stunning effect. His hand went to his hip, seeking the six-gun that wasn't there and he uttered a low curse of frustration as Bard came at him once again.

Lane Lester, still cowering against the wall was watching,

not knowing what to do. There came a loud, excited shout from the hall's open doorway.

"Fight! Out here! Fight!"

One of the soldiers had stepped out for air and saw the two men battling in the street. Moments later, others were crowding through the doorway, pausing to watch. Several women also came from the hall. One of them saw Lane standing against the wall and offered a derisive sniff. Meantime, the onlookers were able to identify the two flailing men, but seemed not to know for which man they should be cheering.

"What started it?" someone wanted to know.

"Dunno, but somebody better break it up!"

"Let 'em fight," another suggested. "It's more excitement than the dance."

Sergeant Major Keene had forced his way through the crowded doorway to see what was happening. He hesitated for a moment, then turned back into the drill hall.

In the street, Steve Bard was hammering blows into the gun hawk's face, driving him backward. Gentleman was trying desperately to ward off the blows, but Bard unleashed a powerhouse right that sent his opponent sprawling to the dust. Bard was puffing hard, shoulders heaving, as he stepped forward to glare down at the fallen man. It was several seconds before he was able to catch his breath and speak. When he did, his voice was low-pitched with menace.

"Get up and get out, Gentleman." He glanced at an ill-dressed man who was watching with a scowl. Bard gestured toward the man. "Take your trash with you."

Blood seeping from a cut lip, Gentleman had propped himself up on one elbow. He wiped the lip with a knuckle, glanced at the blood. His eyes were slitted as he looked up at Bard, then slowly began to get to his feet.

The aging sergeant major had bulled his way back

through the crowd and stood on the top step. Gentleman's two six-gun rig was across his shoulder, one of the six-guns still holstered. The other revolver the soldier held in his hand, unloading one chamber at a time, allowing each lead-loaded cartridge to fall on the steps.

The gun unloaded, he shoved it back in its holster, then pulled the rig off his shoulder and tossed it into the street at Gentleman's feet. The gunman bent to pick up the outfit, his hand going to one of the six-guns.

"They're both unloaded," the sergeant major informed him. "Like I said earlier, you'd best get off government property before we throw you in our guard house."

Jim Blade had edged through the crowd and stood near Lane Lester, his bulk tending to shield her from the other onlookers. In one hand, he carried a glass of punch. He was observing the man Bard had spotted earlier as one of Gentleman's people. Blade paused on the veranda, watching the man's eyes. As the man allowed his hand to drop to the butt of a six-gun, Blade shoved the glass of punch toward him.

"Here. Hold this!"

The man, taken by surprise, used his gun hand to grasp the glass; a reflex action. Blade, smiling amiably, jammed his hand inside his coat to bring out a Colt Pocket Pistol. He aimed it at this man who obviously was one of Gentleman's followers, nodding at the glass in the man's hand.

"Take it with you. I hope you've had a good time."

The outlaw glared at Blade for a moment then turned to hurl the glass of liquid down the length of the veranda. It crashed on the wooden floor, glass shattering, as the man moved down the steps and paused beside Gentleman. The gun hawk looked at his follower and jerked his head to indicate a hitch rack where their horses were tied. The man helped

Gentleman to his feet. The pair slowly moved toward their mounts, the gun hawk attempting to hide a limp. Bard walked to the steps, then turned to look after the pair. The sentry at the fort's entrance apparently had surmised what was happening and already was unbarring the gate so he could swing it open.

On the veranda, people were talking in low tones, as Jim Blade turned to face them. He was smiling, but his tone held quiet authority. "It's all over, folks. The musicians want to earn their money so let's all get back to the dancing."

Slowly, the gathering began to drift back into the drill hall and the four-piece band, which had been silent since the fight had started, swung into a familiar tune. Lane Lester was leaning against the wall next to the door. She watched as Bard came up the steps and started to enter the hall. The woman extended her arm to stop him.

"Mr. Bard. Please!" There was a formal note in her tone and Bard halted to stare at her. It was impossible to tell what he was thinking.

"I want to thank you," she said quietly, looking into his face. She shook her head, puzzled. "I don't understand what it's all—"

"It's alright, miss." He was frowning at her final statement. "What is it you don't understand?"

Lane shook her head, still puzzled. "I thought you were like Gentleman. One of Jud Ransom's hired guns."

"Oh?"

"In the bath yesterday, you were saying—"

"In the bath?" Bard interrupted, scowling at her. The woman looked up at him offering a positive nod.

"You were talking about Ransom with someone. Saying how well he's done since the old days. I heard you."

Bard, still scowling, shook his head. "I was alone." Then slow realization softened his expression. "That man,

Howard, and the other one. They came out of the bath house as I was going in."

He bent closer, trying to hide his sudden excitement. "Just what did you hear, Lane?"

It was the first time he had called her by her given name. Surprised at the unexpected familiarity, the girl shook her head.

"Whoever it was said something about Ransom being no more honest now than he was in the old days." She hesitated, trying to recall. "I was lying there in the warm water, half asleep . . . I wasn't really paying attention."

Bard looked away from her, staring toward the gate of the fort where Gentleman and his man were just riding out. The sentry was closing the huge gate behind them.

"What's this all about, Steve?" Lane wanted to know.

Bothered by what he had heard, Steve Bard shook his head. "I don't know, but it's time someone was doin' something to find out."

"Steve, I need to talk to you!"

There was purpose in Jim Blade's voice as he strode across the street, coming from the direction of the gate. Lane glanced at him, then back to Bard.

"I'd better see how the party's going," she declared, turning toward the doorway. Bard watched her go, then turned back to Blade, who had mounted the steps to face him.

"What is it, Jim?"

"I was standing down there near the gate, when Gentleman and that other crud rode out. The guy said something about them being back sooner than we'd think. Gentleman told him to shut up!"

Bard considered the news for a moment, then nodded. "I told Lane it's time someone found out what's going on. I guess it'd best be now. Get your horse."

Chapter Fourteen

Steve Bard drew rein on his horse to halt on the crest of a steep hill. Jim Blade edged his own mount up to stop beside the scout. There was a quarter moon offering enough light with the help of bright starlight to display the valley before them. It was the same area where the two of them had been halted by Jack Gentleman after they had heard firing in the distance. This time, however, they had avoided the trail through the canyon, where they had been stopped. It had been a long uphill climb and the horses were breathing with gasping labor, flanks heaving. Both men loosened their reins, allowing the horses more freedom in catching their breath.

Both rode their own Mexican-style saddles featuring a horn and *tapadero*-covered stirrups rather than the flat cavalry models. To each saddle was attached a military-issue scabbard housing a Model 1866 Winchester carbine. In the dull moonlight, there was still a reflection off of the brass frame of each of the weapons. Bard had awakened a duty armorer at the fort to draw the pair of weapons before they had ridden out in the night.

101

As they sat there, Blade withdrew his carbine from the scabbard and looked it over. Both of the men had loaded up the lever action repeaters' long tubular magazines with .44 rimfire cartridges before leaving the fort. Additional boxed ammo was in their saddlebags. Barrels of the carbines measured twenty inches, four inches shorter than those of the standard infantry rifles. Instead of a steel butt plate, this model carried one of brass. The barrel was round and boasted a polished brown finish produced by a controlled rust process rather than blued octagon barrels that were the standard for most military weapons of the period.

"These have come a long way from the Henry model I carried during the war," Blade commented, keeping his voice low. Both men knew that the Winchester had been upgraded from the Henry rifle, which had been issued to Union troops.

"Who'd you serve with?" Bard wanted to know, eyeing the terrain in front of them. He also spoke in a low tone.

"First District of Columbia Cavalry. I was a sniper for most of my tour."

Blade didn't add that his greatest failure had been a moment in which he had Robert E. Lee in his sights. He was firing from nearly seven hundred yards away. Between the time he pulled the trigger and it took the heavy lead bullet to travel the distance, another officer had stepped in front of General Lee to hand him some papers. The unknown officer had taken the bullet in the spine and had died instantly; Lee had lived to fight more battles . . . and eventually surrender.

Bard chuckled and the journalist cast him a puzzled look. "Something funny?"

Bard shook his head. "No. Just circumstance. We captured a couple of hundred Henry rifles from your outfit back in 1864. They was issued later to us in the 7th Virginia Cavalry."

Bard patted the butt stock of the carbine extending from his scabbard. "I like this one better." He tightened the reins on his horse, pulling up its head. "I doubt Gentleman has a guard posted down there at night, but we won't take a chance. We'll stick to the high ground."

Blade cast him an amused glance. "Any idea where we are?"

Bard nodded. "I looked at some maps before we left. Down below there's where Gentleman faced us down today. Near as I can tell, Ransom's land butts up against the Navajo reservation."

Blade eyed the area below. "You think all that shooting we heard was coming from the Indian's side of the line?"

"Hard to tell, but I'd wager on it." He glanced at the other. "While I was at it, I had the sergeant major show me on the map just where Ransom and his crew hang out. That's where we're headed."

Blade shook his head thoughtfully. "It's possible, you know, that the man I overheard there at the gate was just blowing off steam."

"Possible," the other conceded, "but I'm also somewhat curious about what happened to that Tom Howard and his boys. I heard talk that they rode outa the fort last night with Gentleman."

There was a short pause in the conversation, while each considered the other's expressed thoughts.

"I do have a question about all this," Blade finally stated. "Why'd you invite me along on this little moonlight outing?"

Bard's teeth showed bright in the moonlight, a surprise since he didn't often smile. "I need someone to cover my back. I already know how well you shoot. Besides, you ain't had much to write about up to now. Maybe we'll find somethin' tonight!"

"Thanks for the vote of confidence."

There was a note of sarcasm in Blade's tone, but he didn't know whether Bard heard it. The scout had nudged his horse forward with the rowels of his spurs, expecting the journalist to follow.

Several miles away, the foursome led by Jesse James was encamped in a hollow between the rocks and above the trail. Although not chosen purposely, the boulders tended to furnish cover against a chilly wind. Clell Miller and Jeb Smith were wrapped in their saddle blankets, sleeping, while Frank and Jesse hunkered over the coals of a small fire that had been built before sundown.

"We either go back to the fort for a shoe and horseshoe nails or we go back to Ransom's and steal a fresh horse," Frank muttered, not wanting to awaken the two sleeping men. He glanced toward the edge of the clearing, where the horses of the four men were munching at dry grass. It was Jeb Smith's horse that had thrown a shoe and gone lame, but thus far, there was no thought of leaving him behind.

"Not much we can do this late," Jesse agreed. "Let's wait 'til mornin' and see how the horse does."

"That'll just be delayin' things, Jesse. He might be some better by then, but with all the rocks in these hills, he'll be lame again before noon."

"Get some sleep, Frank," Jesse instructed. "I'll keep watch for awhile, then you can take over. We'll figure it out in daylight."

"If we go back to th' fort, folks'll want to know where we've been," Frank pointed out as he rose.

"And if we try to steal a horse from Ransom, we might get killed. He didn't much like the way we pulled out of whatever fracas he's got planned."

Instead of moving to where his saddle and blankets were

laid out, Frank edged to where the picketed horses stood. He bent to grasp one of the picket lines to where it was staked, then followed the length of rope to one of the haltered horses that was grazing. Laying a hand on the horse's neck, he spoke to it quietly. The horse raised his head, bending his neck to look at the man.

Frank James continued to speak quiet, soothing words to the animal as he bent to pick up its left front foot, lifting the hoof to inspect it in what was left of the moonlight. The shoe was missing and the hoof was ragged, worn down to the tender area called the frog in the center. The train robber fingered the pastern area above the hoof, feeling the fever and swelling that he detected beneath the hair. He shook his head and allowed the horse to drop the foot to the ground. He turned to look at his brother, still keeping his voice low.

"Jesse, that horse ain't going nowhere tomorrow, shod or not."

At the fort, a sentry slumped against the wall adjoining the high gate, attempting to fight off sleepiness. Music still issued from the drill hall, but it was a slower tune now, almost a dirge, devoid of the evening's earlier merriment.

Lane Lester stood on the veranda that fronted the hall, watching as some of the settlers crossed the street that divided the permanent buildings from their encampment. They seemed to move as slowly as the music they could still hear, physically spent by the evening's activities.

Frowning, Lane wondered what had happened to Captain Jackson. Someone said he had gone to his quarters after a discussion with Steve Bard. He had not come back. He had boasted that the party would last until dawn, but it looked as though he had been the first to fold.

Lane also found she was thinking of Bard and Blade, wondered what had become of them. Like the captain, they had simply disappeared from the festivities. Curious, she had approached the sentry on the gate at midnight, as the watch was changing. She had been told by the man going off duty that the two had ridden out of the fort more than an hour earlier.

The blond woman turned to look through the open doorway to the drill hall floor, where a few of the younger people were still dancing, fighting off their weariness, seeking to take full advantage of a celebration they did not expect to see repeated any time soon in the days ahead. Lane stifled a yawn and wondered whether the captain had been serious about keeping the dance going until dawn. If so, he should have been the one who stayed to see it through.

Determined, she entered the hall and walked to the far end, where the four musicians still played, although their heads were hanging. She waited until the tune was ended, then approached the oldster with the fiddle.

"It's time to close down, Lem. You're all about to fall on your face. Give them one more dance, then pack up."

The weary man's eyes brightened at the news. He stood up, rapping on the back of his fiddle with his knuckles to gain attention. Some of the dancers had drifted to the table where the punch and sandwiches had been laid out only to find that both food and drink were long gone. They turned to listen to the fiddler.

"Last dance coming up, folks. We've just about wore our fingers down to the knuckle tonight and it's time we was all under the blankets."

Surprising to Lane Lester, there were no spoken complaints from the seven couples still on the floor. In fact, several of the settlers nodded agreement. The soldiers who had taken part in the festivities had long since found their bunks.

Lane had brought a shawl into the hall before the festivities began. She took it down from the wall hook where she had hung it earlier and draped it over her shoulders as she headed for the doorway. She felt perhaps she should be staying until all of the couples had left, but she also felt that should have been Captain Jackson's responsibility. After all, it was his fort and for the present, his command; the dance had been his idea. He had hinted that she would be paid for her efforts, but that was all it had been: a hint. She heaved a sigh, realizing that such negative thoughts no doubt were being generated by her weariness. Actually, she had been surprised when several of the wives had paused to congratulate her on how well she had planned the party.

On the veranda she halted, glancing all around, half expecting Jack Gentleman to appear. There was nobody. She was bone weary as she managed the steps and began to walk toward the encampment and the covered wagon that had become her home.

Jack Gentleman was nowhere near the fort. Now less than half a mile ahead of Bard and Blade, he was approaching the guarded gate that led to the buildings of the Ransom rancho. The guard recognized him and the outlaw who had ridden with him from Fort Wingate. The gate was open for the pair, as their horses reached it. The gun hawk allowed the other man to pass through, then pulled up his horse to look down at the guard.

"Anything happened?" he wanted to know. He had noticed that lights were on in the main house where Ransom lived. The guard offered a shrug.

"Not much. That big Injun rode in 'bout an hour ago. Said he was here to see the boss."

Gentleman looked toward the big house and saw the markings of the pinto horse Long Arm always rode. As his companion headed for the corral to unsaddle and turn out his horse, Gentleman spurred his own mount toward the hitch rack in front of the house where he dismounted and looped his reins over the rail beside the Indian's pinto.

Bard and Blade had approached to within fifty yards of the guarded gate and were able to see what was happening in the thin moonlight. They both noticed the big pinto tied beside Gentleman's horse, but the lighted window was of more interest.

"Looks like Ransom's got a late visitor," Bard muttered beneath his breath.

Inside, the door to Ransom's office stood open and Gentleman could see Long Arm standing before the rancher's desk, back toward the door. He entered without knocking and halted beside the Indian, casting him a glance. This was the first time Ransom had ever allowed any Indian inside the house. Something had to be coming down!

Ransom had been lighting one of his cigars from a thin twig he had set ablaze in the fireplace, where the fire was burning down. He looked up to glare at his gun hawk.

"I send you out to get information and you come back lookin' like you've been guest of dishonor at a lynch party!"

Gentleman straightened at the comment, scowling, then dropped his eyes to look at his attire. One shirtsleeve was nearly torn off, his trousers were torn and dirty. Somewhere along the way, he had lost his hat. The marks of the beating he had taken were on his face. He cast Ransom a resentful glance as he raised his eyes. Beside him, the Indian was looking him over, but one could read nothing from his expression.

"I learned what you wanted to know," Gentleman announced. "Most of them soldiers'll be worn out from an all-night dance. Two troops are out patrollin' reservation boundaries. We could probably walk in without much of a fight."

Ransom stared at his man for a long moment, his cigar forgotten. He was still staring at Gentleman, when he spoke.

"What do you think, Long Arm?"

The Navajo eyed Gentleman for a moment longer, then took a step closer to the desk, looking at Ransom. He said nothing until the rancher took the hint and rose to his feet, figuratively putting them on an equal footing. The Indian offered a nod of approval or acceptance. "Good plan. Attack at dawn. Soldiers all full with whiskey, still sleepy. They no fight. Easy!"

Chapter Fifteen

Steve Bard and Jim Blade were lying on their bellies at the edge of a thicket roughly a hundred yards from the ranch house. The shambling figure guarding the gate was no more than half that distance from where the two of them lay. Bard was watching the house through an old military spyglass he always carried in his saddlebags. Through the large window that looked out from Jud Ransom's office, he could see the tall Indian standing in front of a desk. Although he could not see the man from where he lay, Bard was certain the Indian was talking to Ransom. The scout also was relatively certain the redskin was Long Arm, who was said to lead the band of reservation jumpers that had been causing all the trouble.

After several minutes of study, including a long look at the gate guard, he handed the small telescope to Blade, who adjusted it to his own vision, then looked toward the lighted window. The window was only dimly lit by several tallow candles that no doubt had been made on the ranch from cattle that had been butchered for food. He noted that smoke was issuing from the house's chimney, which would explain the flickering of firelight as well as illumination from the candles.

110

"I'd give a good saddle to know what's going on down there right now," Bard whispered.

Blade lowered the glass to glance at him for an instant, then began inspecting the scene through the lenses once more. "I can use a good saddle," the journalist finally announced, handing the glass back to Bard and starting to rise to his knees. The scout reached over to pull him back to his belly, shaking his head.

"You don't get paid to scout, Jim. I do. I'll try to get around that gate guard and see what's up," Bard announced. "You stay here and cover me with the Winchesters." The two of them had been thoughtful enough to leave their horse back in the trees and bring the .44 rimfire carbines with them to the edge of the trees.

Blade shook his head. "As a guest, I should have my choice of chores," he hissed, wanting to press his point without alerting the guard.

Bard didn't choose to argue. Instead, he slid his own long gun across the leaves so it was within Blade's reach.

"I hope you don't need this one, too," he whispered, then backed away, still on his belly.

In the ranch house, Ransom, Gentleman and Long Arm had been discussing tactics.

"Me and my men'll make it easy for you, Long Arm. We'll ride into the fort and I'll say I've decided we'll help defend it like that fool captain wants. Once we're inside, we can take out the sentry and open the gate for your warriors."

"We want rifles. How many we get?" the Indian demanded.

"The new '73 Winchesters came in by supply wagon a couple of weeks back, but they ain't been issued yet. There're a hundred twenty troopers in the outfit, so that means that many new rifles.

"They've been waitin' for the other two troops to come back from patrols to issue them all at once. There'll be the extra Model '66 rifles they're got now, plus whatever arms you'll get from them settlers camped there." The rancher offered a nod to emphasize his words. "You should get plenty of ammunition, too."

Long Arm thought about what had been said for a long moment, then offered a decisive nod.

"We get soldier rifles. Kill soldiers. Kill settlers. No more come." He shook his head to emphasize his approach to the problem. "Afraid."

Jud Ransom nodded his head with a false enthusiasm. Long Arm was making the whole project sound too simple.

"With the soldiers all dead, we just raid the armory. You help me keep th' homesteaders out of this country and I'll help you get a lot more rifles. Lots of munitions, too," he promised.

"There's only one thing I want out of this," Jack Gentleman announced quietly, eyeing his boss. "Beyond my usual pay, of course."

Ransom eyed his gun hawk, wondering what kind of demand was being made. "What's that, Jack?"

"I want that cavalry scout's scalp!"

Outside, Bard had made a big circle around the guard at the gate, coming into the ranch compound from behind the horse corral. Some of the horses held in the enclosure had moved about, disturbed by his presence, but he stood quiet for several minutes, waiting for them to settle down before he scuttled across the open area to take up a post beneath the lighted window.

Slowly, the scout raised his head, looking into the room through a lower corner of the glass window. Long Arm, still standing in front of Ransom's desk, had his arms folded across his buckskin-clad chest. Gentleman stood a step or two behind the Indian. Ransom was standing, but frowned as he slowly lowered his bulk into his chair. He shook his head, frowning. Despite the thickness of the glass, Bard could hear his words.

"I wish I knew where them James boys are tonight." Ransom glanced at Gentleman. "You didn't see them? They weren't at the fort?" He was worried that Jesse and Frank might have tipped off the cavalry as to what was in the wind, although they couldn't possibly know much about his plans.

Gentleman shook his head. "No sign of them. We can handle things without any help from them."

That comment did little to soothe Ransom's concern. "It isn't that. It's just that no one's ever certain what they're goin' to do. Especially Jesse. He's erratic as hell!"

Steve Bard heard the exchange, wondering. It was obvious that Jesse James, the bank and train robber, was being discussed.

"Jesse James, Tom Howard or anything else he calls himself makes no difference. I can take him. His brother, too."

Gentleman's words came as a revelation to Bard. The men he had ridden with from Silver Hill were members of the James gang, all four of them with prices on their heads. He had been aware that the quartet had disappeared from the fort with Gentleman, but this was the first inkling as to the real identities of the outlaw band.

The scout leaned closer to the window, trying to hear what was being said in lowered tones. He peeked over the ledge and watched as Jud Ransom reached to a pewter cup on his desk, where several twigs of perhaps eight inches in length stood upright. He selected one of the twigs and turned toward the fireplace and lit it from the flames. He then used the bit of wood to relight a cigar that apparently had gone out. The procedure accomplished, he threw the burning twig into the flames and turned back to the others.

"Don't try nothin'!"

The voice came from directly behind Bard and he started slowly elevating his hands, wondering what had happened to Blade, his backup the back of his neck.

"Get up now," came the order. "Real slow like, hands in the air."

As the scout followed the man's demands, he felt the Single Action Army Colt being lifted from his holster. There was a minor crashing sound, as the weapon was tossed into a decorative bush that had been planted against the wall of the house.

"Head for the door, mister," Bard's captor ordered, lowering the gun barrel until it was pressed against the scout's spine. The ruckus outside the window had attracted attention from those inside. As he turned toward the front of the door a dozen feet away, Bard saw Gentleman step to the window, staring through it, trying to see what was happening. The tall Indian stepped up beside the gunman, shading his eyes against the light in the room to peer into the darkness.

At the door to the house, Bard halted, hands still in the air.

"Open it," his captor ordered. "Use your left hand. No tricks or I'll separate your backbone."

Moving carefully, Bard lowered the designated hand to grasp the doorknob and twist it, then shoved the door open.

"Get that hand up, again." The man behind him was being totally cautious, Bard noted. The gun muzzle was still against his spine, as he was pushed through a semi-dark room that received some light from the open door leading to what Ransom used as an office.

As he crossed the threshold into the office, Bard pretended to stumble, going almost to his knees. Had his captor fired, he would have been shooting at Jack Gentleman. Bard deliberately fell against the gun hawk, making a grab for one of the holstered six-guns on the other's belt. While he wrestled to draw the gun, one of Gentleman's hands holding against the effort, the gun hawk managed to drag the other revolver from its holster and he used its barrel to slash Bard across the back of his neck. The scout folded, sprawling on the floor. A gun suddenly in each hand, Gentleman stepped forward to kick Bard in the ribs several times. Each time showed increased visciousness, as he cursed the semiconscious man.

"That's enough, Jack!" Ransom's order was loud and harsh. "Don't kill him yet!"

As Gentleman hesitated, then took a step to the rear, the man who had captured Bard pushed forward, his six-gun still clutched in his hand.

"He got around the guard on the gate. Came in from behind our corral," the man volunteered, looking for praise or at least approval. "I seen him and waited 'til he got to the window. He was listenin' to whatever you all had to say."

Ransom cast the man a nod. "He probably didn't expect you to be watchin' the house. You did good, but you'd best get back out there. He might not be alone."

As the man holstered his gun and made for the door, Bard stirred. He was lying face down, but slowly managed to arch his back and crawl to his hands and knees. He shook his head and uttered a groan. His hat brim had softened some of the strength of the gun barrel swung at him by Gentleman.

"Get him up!" Ransom ordered, looking at Gentleman. The rancher motioned to the chair facing his desk. "Set him there!"

The gun hawk grabbed Bard roughly by the shoulders and jerked him to his feet. Another groan of pain came from the disoriented scout, but went ignored as he was shoved into the chair. During this, Long Arm had stepped to the side of the room and was watching with open interest, although he was scowling.

With Bard lolling in the chair, chin against his chest, Ransom stepped forward to grab the front of his shirt and jerk him upright. He then grabbed him by the chin and forced the head back until he was looking into the scout's pain-dulled eyes.

"How many of them Winchester rifles are at the fort?" Ransom wanted to know. "The new repeaters. The 1873s. Where've they got them stored?"

With the grip he had on Bard's chin, Ransom realized it was almost impossible for the man to talk. He jerked his hand away, glaring down at the other. Bard was quickly recovering his senses. He shook his head and offered a grimace at the pain created by the effort.

"You should've caught a quartermaster sergeant, not an Indian scout, mister."

"Where are those guns? In the armory?"

Bard only returned the rancher's glare, saying nothing. Ransom turned abruptly to the fireplace beside his desk. He bent to look at the flames, then picked out a partially burned stick that had a smoldering coal at one end. He inspected the coal for an instant, then held it closer to his face, blowing on the glowing coal. It brightened under the induced draught and he straightened, satisfied.

"Now, Jack, if you'll deprive this man of his shirt . . ."

Panicked at what was about to take place, Bard started to rise, trying to get out of the chair, but Gentleman slammed him back against the leather upholstery, drawing a gun with his other hand.

"Get it off!" he demanded. "A bullet in the belly's just as painful and lot more fatal!"

Bard hesitated for a moment, glancing at each of the white men in turn, then staring for a moment at the Indian.

Gentlemen jabbed at his wishbone with the muzzle of the six-gun.

"Now!"

Bard slowly undid the elk horn buttons and leaned forward to slip his arms out of the sleeves of the buckskin. Gentleman grabbed the jacket and hurled it into the fire, where it smoldered for a moment, then burst into flame. As Ransom and the gunman watched the blaze, Bard turned his eyes upon the Indian who had been standing near the door, observing.

"Long Arm, what're you getting' out of this except more grief for your people?" the scout asked, scowling. It was an effort for him to speak.

Gentleman stepped closer to Bard, baring his teeth, as he raised his revolver as though to strike the prisoner across the face with the cold metal.

"No!" Long Arm spoke from where he stood, arms still folded across his chest. "Let him speak."

Gentleman looked to Ransom for guidance, but the rancher was staring at the Indian, eyes narrowed. Bard took advantage of the silence.

"This man's usin' you, Long Arm. All he wants is the gold in these hills." He jerked his head to indicate Ransom. "You'll fight for him and your people'll die. When you need his help, he'll laugh at you or send the cavalry to run you down!"

Bard turned to glare at Ransom. "I know about the gold. You paid off Kalispell Kane in nuggets. Captain Jackson knows about it, too. You'll have the whole United States Army on your back if you start an Indian war!"

The Indian said nothing, only stared down at the face of the scout, but Bard thought he saw a hint of disgust at the way things were being handled. Long Arm probably was wondering why this white man wasn't already dead.

Standing behind him, Gentleman suddenly wrapped his hands about Bard's throat, jerking him back into the chair. Bard clawed at the fingers cutting of his breathing, but the gunman's fingers were like cables. Ransom, the burning timber in hand, stepped closer, ready to ram it into the scout's chest.

"Last chance, mister. Talk or suffer."

Bard's features were twisted in agony, but his mouth was clamped shut as the torch was jammed into his chest. The scout twisted about, trying to get away from the fire that was searing its way into his flesh. Finally, he could hold out no longer and his mouth opened to emit a scream of pain. With his air supply cut off by Gentleman's grip, all that came out was a stifled moan.

Chapter Sixteen

As Jud Ransom drew back, removing the burning brand from Bard's chest, a raw, sooty burn was visible in the man's flesh.

"That's enough, Jack. Don't kill him before I get some answers."

Gentleman loosened his hold on Bard's throat and the scout's head fell forward in seeming unconsciousness. Gentleman grabbed his hair and pulled his head back. Bard slowly opened his eyes, mouth twisting in a grimace of pain. Ransom stared down at the man, still holding the smoking length of wood.

"This time we'll go for an eye, Bard. How do you think you'll do as a scout with one eye gone? Or maybe both of them?"

Eighty yards away, Jim Blade lay in the darkness, staring toward the flickering lights he could see in the house. He had tried to follow Bard's progress in bypassing the guard on the compound's gate, but had lost him in the darkness. He picked up the spyglass the scout had left and concentrated on the ranch house window, but all he could see was a tall Indian standing in what appeared to be the middle of the room. There was no sign of Bard, but it was likely that he was moving slowly and hadn't had time to reach the structure.

Blade heaved a sigh and laid aside the glass. He offered an almost silent chuckle as he wondered what he was doing there, lying on his belly in the middle of the night, with a Winchester rifle on either side of him.

There was only the one Indian pony tied at the rail, but there probably were more renegade Indians somewhere close by. Jack Gentleman had to be in the house, too. His horse was tied beside the big black and white pinto that no doubt belonged to the Indian he had seen through the glass.

He had been in his last year at Yale, when the Confederacy had fired on Fort Sumter and started the War Between the States. He had quit seeking an education to enlist in the Union Army as a private. He had been through half a dozen battles by the time the war ended, building a reputation as an expert marksman and sniper.

After being discharged, he had returned to Yale, but hadn't lasted a semester. Bored to distraction, he had quit and headed for New York. In spite of the horrors he had seen during his war years, he missed the action and intrigue. He missed the excitement.

Based more upon his education than experience, he had taken a job as a reporter on the *New York Times*. He had covered police activities and the local crime scene for more than two years, before he had occasion to sit beside the *Times* founding editor, Horace Greeley at a political luncheon he was covering.

It became obvious during that interlude that Greeley was aware the young reporter worked for him but that he knew nothing about him beyond the fact that he had been educated at Yale.

Blade had heard frequent references to the fact that

Greeley had made a trip overland from New York to California in the days before the Civil War had started. He had returned to declare that the future of young America was not in the eastern cities but in the west. His suggestion to one of his reporters, "Go West, young man," had been quoted often enough for the entire *Times* staff to be familiar with it.

Covering police and crime activities, Blade had found a sameness to happenings and his resulting news reports often were less than inspiring. That chance meeting at the politically inspired luncheon had suggested to Blade a new approach. He had waited several days before requesting an audience with the editor/publisher, then had suggested that he be given a roving assignment in the west. It eventually was agreed that rather than a salary, he would be paid space rates—so much a column inch—for the frontier reports that were published in Greeley's newspaper. As an afterthought, he also asked for the right to do articles for *Harper's Weekly* and other publications that did not compete directly with the *Times*. It usually took the checks weeks, sometimes even months, to catch up with him in his wanderings, but he had managed a reasonably comfortable living.

One of Blade's first big stories involved the court martial of Brevet General George Armstrong Custer at Fort Leavenworth, Kansas on multiple charges born of an unauthorized absence at Fort Wallace, Kansas.

According to evidence presented at the court martial, Custer and his men had just returned to Fort Wallace from a long and exhaustive march. The men and officers were tired and the horses out of condition, but the commanding officer had ordered three officers and seventy-five troopers to accompany him to Fort Harker, a distance of nearly three hundred miles, so he could see his wife.

According to legal specifications duly reported by Blade, while en route, a segment of Custer's party was attacked by hostile Indians. When the attack was over, it was charged, Custer had neglected to pursue the Indians and made no effort to recover the bodies of two of his soldiers who had been killed in the Indian attack.

It was further charged that at one point, three men had attempted to desert Custer's column. He had ordered three officers to fire upon them. All three enlisted men were wounded, one man later dying from the effects of a bullet. It was further charged that the three had been placed in a government wagon and refused medical treatment on Custer's order.

Custer had been found guilty of all charges. The court martial board stripped him of his rank of brevet general, returning him to his permanent rank of lieutenant colonel. He also was suspended from command for a year, with forfeit of pay for the same length of time.

It had always amazed Blade that at the end of his suspension, Custer once again took command of the same unit, the Seventh Cavalry Regiment.

During these travels, Jim Blade had come across several women he found both attractive and desirable, but none of them had been interested in following him in his nomadic career.

The arrangement had worked well until 1872, when Greeley had died. The new management of the *Times* had dispensed with Blade's services, but the nomadic journalist had continued to write for *Harper's* and other major newspapers.

In pondering the course that had brought him to this thicket somewhere in New Mexico, Blade's thoughts were fleeting and fragmented, some of them dark, others like flashes of light. Lying there, attempting to see what was happening in the house on the low hill beyond the corral, he also found himself wondering what Lane Lester was doing at that moment. With luck, she should be deep in sleep like normal human beings. Chance were, he realized, that was not happening. It had been apparent that the settlers and even some of the soldiers at the fort had thought that Steve Bard and Gentleman had been battling over the woman. That supposition certainly wasn't going to improve her reputation.

Blade's attention was drawn suddenly to the scene he had been watching. There seemed to be sudden movement inside the house. He groped for the spyglass, finding it with his hand and centering it on the lighted rectangle of the large window. There was sufficient light for him to see that Steve Bard had been taken captive. It was difficult for him to make out exactly what was happening, since the partial moon had dropped behind the mountains. It appeared, though, that Bard was being marched to the front door of the house. There was light when the door was opened and he was able to see the scout, hands aloft, marched into the structure at gunpoint. The door closed behind him and his captor.

Blade laid aside the spyglass and grabbed the carbine that had been issued to him. Carefully, so as not to alert the man guarding the gate of the compound, he pulled down the lever, then shoved it up, thus inserting a cartridge in the weapon's chamber. He watched the man guarding the gate until he was certain the mechanical clicking of the loading procedure had not carried that far.

Looking through the spyglass once more, Blade could see through the window. Steve Bard, his buckskin shirt gone, was seated in a chair, with Gentleman behind him, seeming to choke him.

Jud Ransom approached the prisoner with the smoking brand, waving it in front of him, seeming to make demands.

Bard writhed in the chair as Ransom jammed the white-hot stick against his bare chest.

Blade muttered a curse and dropped the glass, grabbing the rifle and bringing it to his shoulder. As he attempted to get a bead on Ransom's form without endangering the scout, a dark image suddenly blocked out some of his vision of the scene.

He had been taking up slack in the trigger before the figure materialized and the bullet was on the way with a sharp cracking sound. The gate guard swung toward him and Blade leveled on him, firing once more. The man dropped.

Inside the house, there was pandemonium. The man who had taken Bard prisoner had been curious enough that he had drifted back to the window to watch the proceedings within. Shocked at what he saw, he had risen to his full height just in time to take Jim Blade's .44 rimfire bullet through his neck. He was dead before he hit the ground.

It had been the sound of breaking glass that had created sudden panic in the room. Gentleman released his hold on Bard and whirled, trying to draw his six-guns. Long Arm had dropped to his belly on the floor, eyes narrowed, as he glanced about, seeking the source of the shooting. Ransom had dropped the burning branch and had turned to his desk, clawing for a weapon that wasn't there.

Steve Bard sat in the chair for a long moment, as surprised as everyone else. But he also realized this was his one chance. In spite of the burning pain in his flesh, he rocketed to his feet, hitting Gentleman with his shoulder as he ran. The gunman was thrown off balance and a shot from one of his six-guns went into the ceiling.

The big window was partially broken, pieces of jagged glass still hanging from parts of the frame. Bard saw the dangers but ignored them as he hurled himself headfirst through the window.

As he tucked his body to land on his shoulders in the grass outside, he rolled toward the bush where his captor had tossed his six-gun. Desperately, he clawed the ground beneath the greenery. Suddenly, the Army Colt was in his hand and he was on his knees, whirling toward the window.

Jack Gentleman was framed against the flickering light from inside. In each hand, he had a six-gun and was peering into the night. Less than ten feet from the gun hawk, Bard raised his own revolver, thumbed back the hammer and fired in what could have been interpreted as a single motion. Gentleman sagged, trying to draw himself erect. A second shot from Bard's Colt sent him backward into the room.

Bard paused for a moment, overcome with pain from the burn he had suffered, but he was still eyeing the window, hoping to see Ransom. There was no sign of either him or Long Arm. Meantime, shouts were coming from the bunkhouse and the scout could see half-dressed men streaming out the door. Most of them were in their long underwear, but that didn't mean they didn't have guns.

Heaving to his feet, Bard ran, half stumbling, toward the hitch rack, where Gentleman's horse and the Indian pony were tied. The pinto was closest and he jerked the slip knot to free the horse's rope war bridle, hauling himself onto the horse's blanketed back.

He still had his six-gun in his hand, but managed to control the rope reins with the other as he whirled the animal and sent it down the hill toward the thicket where Blade was hidden. There was firing from behind him. Bard knew that the pinto's white markings were a giveaway, but he also saw flashes from the Winchester up ahead of him. Blade was attempting to cover his escape.

He was within yards of the thicket, when he heard the

thump of a bullet hitting his mount. It had to have been a deadly shot, for the horse suddenly fell out from under him and he was rolling into the underbrush, the bushes clawing at his chest wound.

Chapter Seventeen

Jud Ransom's band of renegades, most aroused from sleep and in their underwear, was totally disorganized. Those clutching guns fired toward the dead pinto that lay in front of the thicket where Steve Bard and Jim Blade lay. The two men could hear bullets thunking into the animal's near-lifeless body. One or more of the bullets fired from near the bunkhouse put an end to the animal's suffering. Thankfully, Bard and Blade were hunkered behind the black and white hulk and thus protected.

Ransom and Long Arm had come running from the house, the rancher waving at the twenty or so men who were spread out across the ranch yard. "Knock it off, you idiots!" Ransom shouted angrily. "You're wastin' lead!"

The sounds of firing died slowly. When Bard had landed in the brush, he had been less than five feet from Jim Blade. On his knees, the journalist had grabbed him by his gun belt and dragged him behind the downed pinto. Blade then scrambled back to his original position to grab the two carbines and the spyglass.

Bard lay on his side protected by the pinto's hulk. On his knees, Blade bent over him. "You're still alive, aren't you?"

"More or less," came the strangled reply. Bard slowly sat up, brushing the hair out of his eyes. Somewhere he had lost his hat. He didn't remember where. Cautiously, he looked over the top of the dead animal to see what was happening around the ranch house. Ransom stood in front of the house with the tall Indian, waving his arms at his motley crew. "Saddle your horses and get your rifles!" Ransom shouted at the men. Most of them had lowered their handguns and were staring at him, puzzled, not really knowing what had happened.

"We work for Jack," one of them announced, tone sullen. "Where's he?"

"Gentleman's dead. You work for me now, so move, dammit!"

"I could kill him from here," Blade suggested, reaching for his Winchester.

"No. We'd best get out of here before they get organized," was Bard's reply. "Even with Ransom dead, maybe even the Indian, what about the other tribesmen? They want those guns. They'll come after them!"

In the ranch yard, there was another moment of hesitation before several of the gunslingers turned toward the bunkhouse, muttering between themselves. The others reluctantly turned to follow.

Bard and Blade overheard the exchanges and saw what was happening. Bard glanced at the journalist. "I think it's time to haul ass out of here."

"Actually, it was probably time ten minutes ago," Blade agreed, as he handed the spyglass to Bard, then scooped up both rifles. He glanced at the scout, worried. "Can you make it okay?"

"I'll make it." Bard offered a grim nod. The two turned, half standing, to make their way through the thicket to where their horses were tied. Both were silently praying that stray rounds from the renegades' fusillade of hot lead had not harmed either animal.

"There's no shootin' from there. They must've had horses hid back in the brush." Ransom's voice was snarl. He and Long Arm were standing alone near the hitch rack, when the former made the observation. He turned suddenly to face the Indian, scowling. "We're gonna have to move fast, Long Arm. There's only one troop at the fort now, but chances are that scout is on his way to tell them we're gonna attack."

He shook his head. "Things're movin' faster than I'd planned, so we have to do it before those troops patrolling the reservation boundaries learn what's what and come back to defend the fort."

The Indian said nothing. Instead, he simply stared at Ransom.

"I'll get you a horse and you round up your people. We'll meet at dawn, where those two trails cross 'bout two miles north of the fort. You know the place?"

Long Arm nodded. "I know." There was a moment of hesitation before he asked, "The gold. It means much to you?"

The question caught Ransom by surprise. For an instant, he didn't know how to answer. He finally nodded, looking the Indian in the eye.

"Yes, it does. It means much to me just as freedom from the blue bellies means much to you and your people. Workin' together, we can both get what we want. Understand what I'm sayin'?"

The Indian continued to stare at him for a long moment. Finally, he broke eye contact and offered a nod. "Understand."

Relieved at Long Arm's answer, Ransom glanced toward the corral, where two of his men were catching up mounts. "Good. Let's get you a horse."

Long Arm motioned toward the horse Gentleman had been riding. "I have horse. That one."

It was a magnificent animal that Ransom had ridden himself until Gentleman had threatened to leave if the horse wasn't turned over to him. The animal was a cross of Thoroughbred and Morgan. The blood of the first gave the big animal plenty of speed, the Morgan heritage meaning stability and a tenacity that made him a prize.

"That horse's tired. You don't want him," the rancher told the Indian. "He's plum wore out."

"My horse now," the Indian declared, glancing down the hill to where the mottled pattern of the black and white pinto was visible. "I go."

Without another word, he turned and strode to the horse, loosing the rein that had been looped around the horizontal pole. Not using the stirrups, he swung into the saddle. As he gathered the reins, he looked once more to where Ransom stood, scowling.

"Th' trail crossin' at dawn, Long Arm!" he called. The Indian glanced to where men, now fully clothed and armed, were streaming from the bunkhouse. He cast Ransom a final look, offering a nod as he reined the horse about. He tightened his heels on the horse's flanks, thus urging it to a ground-eating gallop. Ransom glared after him. He knew he was going to have to kill the Indian before this mess was ended. As Long Arm and his mount disappeared in the darkness, the renegade leader glanced once more toward the ranch house. He tried not to admit it, but it bothered him that he wouldn't have Jack Gentleman to back him up.

"Hurry it up!" he shouted. "That scout's hurt, but we got to catch him before he gets to the fort!" Most of the hired gun hands didn't know what he was talking about, but they increased the speed with which they slapped saddles on the backs of the horses and jerked tight the cinches.

"Catch me up a horse!" Ransom yelled. "A good one!"

One man who had just jammed a rifle into a saddle scabbard tied his horse to the corral fence and grabbed a lariat to rope another mount. Satisfied that he'd have a horse, Ransom turned back to his house. Moments later, when he entered the office, he made a point of ignoring the twisted body of Jack Gentleman. Blood from the man's wounds was staining a beautifully woven Navajo rug.

He jerked open the drawer of his desk to pull out a gun belt that carried a cap-and-ball six-round revolver. He checked to be certain each of the nipples on the cylinder had a copper cap pinched in place. This was the same weapon he had carried a decade earlier, when he rode with Quantrill. He hadn't worn the gun in years and noted that the belt needed two extra notches to fit around his middle.

He was on the way out of the room, when he paused. After an instant, he removed the ancient pistol from its holster and dropped it on a chair. One of Jack Gentleman's more modern six-guns was lying next to the body. With barely a glance at the twisted features of his late confederate, he picked up the Smith & Wesson Russian model revolver and hefted it, then shoved it into the holster. In talking to Gentleman, he had learned that more than 20,000 of the guns had been made for the Russian army under a special contract. Only a few thousand had been sold in the United States. The gun hawk had been proud of the guns and nursed them as a mother might a child. This one was bright and clean.

Ransom didn't bother to open the loading gate and check whether the revolver was loaded. He knew Gentleman always loaded all six cylinders, not leaving one empty for the hammer to rest in as a safety measure. He hesitated, then bent over to unbuckle the dead gun slinger's pistol belt and strip it from beneath him. He'd probably need the ammunition carried in the belt loops.

The night was dark, with only the brightness of the Western stars helping to light the trail Bard and Blade had found. They slowed the pace of their horses as they entered a familiar looking cleft in the rocks. As Bard held up his hand in signal for a halt, Blade urged his horse up beside the other animal. He sat staring ahead in the same direction as Bard.

"This is where Gentleman stopped us the other day," Bard declared, voice little more than a whisper. "I'd guess this cut probably has a guard, if they're so bent on keepin' people clear."

"Maybe we ought to backtrack a bit and take the high ground like before."

Bard shook his head, still staring into the darkness ahead. "We'd lose too much time. We gotta ride right on through. Fast!"

Before he could lift his reins, Blade's horse suddenly raised his head and uttered a night-splitting whinny. A second later, the equine's greeting was answered by another horse somewhere down the trail.

"Damn! That takes care of being sneaky," Blade muttered. Bard didn't answer. Instead, he gripped his reins and drove his spurs against his horse's flank. An instant later, Blade followed suit. Both riders bent low over the necks of their surprised, hard-running mounts.

As the two of them raced through the narrow cleft, the sound of a shot echoed off the canyon walls along with the scream of a ricochet. Bard, in the lead, half-expected his horse to drop, but the animal didn't slacken its pace. Then came another shot.

"Two of them!" Blade shouted, there being no further need for silence. There came two more shots before Bard's horse suddenly dropped from under him. In a desperate move to keep from being pinned under the falling animal, he kicked his feet free of the stirrups and levered himself out of the saddle. Behind him, Blade had pulled his own horse into a rear and was squeezing off six-gun shots at a dark figure on the edge of the cliff overlooking the trail.

The man started to fall, the rifle flung from his hands, but Blade didn't wait to see more. He spurred forward to where Bard was groveling in the broken rock, trying to get to his feet. The sharp edges of the stone had cut him in several places on his shoulders and back. Bard's horse was getting to its feet, snorting at the unexpected excitement.

"He ain't hit. He just tripped," Bard shouted. He ran as fast as his battered body would allow, mounting and again driving the spurs home. On the cliff, the remaining guard was having trouble with his rifle, attempting to clear a jam. As Bard and Blade galloped through the narrow confines of the canyon, the guard turned to stare in the direction from which the pair had come. He heard more horses approaching. In the east, the sky was beginning to lighten.

At the fort, neither Lane Lester nor Captain Jackson had enjoyed much sleep. It was coming on five o'clock with the sun not too far behind the eastern mountains, when Sergeant Major Keene knocked on the door of the officer's quarters to tell him what had transpired at the dance after the captain had left.

It was early, but the troops were already up. The horses had been fed and the enlisted men were headed for the mess hall. The old soldier knew his captain should be awake in spite of the early hour.

"I wasn't feeling well, last night," the captain explained to the old soldier. "I just came back here and went to bed."

With Keene knocking on his door, he had managed to get into the uniform trousers he had worn for the dance, then slip a pair of Indian-made elk hide moccasins on his feet. The sergeant major was a veteran of hundreds of military bashes and had watched the captain sampling the punch bowl with uncommon frequency. No wonder he'd made for his bed early.

In making his verbal report, the old cavalryman attempted to pass over the battle between Bard and Jack Gentleman, but Jackson didn't buy his edited version of the physical exchange.

"I don't know which one started it," the sergeant major had said, "but it was pretty obvious who finished it. We run Gentleman and his buddy outa the fort."

"Does the sergeant-of-the-guard have any of this recorded in his log book?" the officer wanted to know. He was frowning and there was a note of anxiety in his tone. Keene offered a nod, understanding his captain's concern and the reasons for it.

"He logged it before I could get to him, sir. Sorry."

Jackson shook his head, frowning. He didn't want the old veteran to know how disturbed he was, but when the colonel returned, he certainly would spend an evening going through the log to determine how things had gone during his absence. Allowing a battle to develop in the street wouldn't look good on his record. It would reflect upon his control of the situation and no doubt be considered a lack of leadership. That's usually the way those things ended up.

As he pondered, Jackson recalled a comment by a senior officer during his days at the U.S. Military Academy at West Point. That individual, in lecturing the young officers-to-be, had pointed out that more military careers were destroyed in the officers club through indiscretions born of alcohol or simply poor social judgment than on the field of battle. The logbook was an official account and it certainly wouldn't do to simply tear out the page or pages that reported the fight. Not that the thought didn't occur to him. Until this moment, he never had so much as pondered what he would do should he be cashiered from the army. It was the only life he knew. His father before him had been an officer who had fought in the Mexican War and had a chest blanketed by medals.

"Where's Bard?" the captain wanted to know. The sergeant major was relieved that the officer wasn't chewing on him for what happened. True, he was the senior enlisted man present, but there still had been a couple of lieutenants there, watching the fight and making no effort to break it up. They'd probably hear from Captain Jackson before the morning became noon.

"I don't know, sir." Keene shook his head. "There was a whole batch of action on th' gate last night. First Gentleman and his man rode out. Not too long after that, Bard and that writer feller saddled up and rode out, too."

"Bard and Jim Blade? Did they say anything about where they were going?"

The sergeant major shook his head. "No, sir. I didn't see 'em go. When I checked th' sentry on the gate, he said they didn't say nothin' to him."

The captain was slipping into his duty blouse as he nodded, still frowning. He offered a tight nod. The obvious answer was that Bard and Blade had been following the gun hawk and the other man.

"Thank you, sergeant major. That will be all. Tell the sergeant of the guard to leave the logbook on my desk. I want to read it."

The sergeant major made his escape, wondering what was

going on in his captain's mind. He made for the mess hall, looking forward to his first cup of coffee for the day. After his more than thirty years of army service, he had learned long ago that coffee was more important to him than the problems of young officers.

Lane Lester was dressed and had groomed her hair as best she could by the light of a candle and a small mirror in her wagon. Instead of the gown she had worn at the dance, she put on a plain dress of rough cotton that she had made out of flour sacks. She had created the garment some years earlier, when she and her brother had been suffering reverses in the gambling business. An enterprising mill had begun packing their flour in specially ordered sacks that carried a printed pattern. There were a number of colored designs, most of them featuring flowers. The problem always had been to lay aside enough empty sacks with the same printed pattern so the finished dress didn't look like a Chinese jigsaw puzzle when finished.

Getting out of the wagon, Lane realized the darkness was thinning around her. Dawn could not be far away. She had no goal as she walked. Her aim was simply to get her mind in some sort of order and try to put aside the unpleasantness of the night before. She had learned long ago that walking helped sort out a jumble of thoughts.

When she had returned to the settlers' camp after the dance, a few of the civilians had been sitting around a campfire. Most had cast her looks, but no one had invited her to join them. She was an outcast, again! At least that was the way she had been made to feel! She did not know that Captain Jackson, emerging from his quarters, was hurrying to overtake her, until she heard his voice behind her.

"Miss Lester, do you know where Mr. Bard and Mr. Blade have gone?"

She halted and turned to face the frowning officer. She shook her head. "I saw them ride out. That's all. It was close to midnight."

"They said nothing to you about where they were going?"

"I have no idea, captain." Her voice was suddenly formal, carrying an edge of ice. "Why would they tell me? Why should you be asking me?" Was the officer blaming her for the fight?

Jackson heaved a sigh. "I told Bard I didn't want any trouble. The settlers were invited to that dance to have fun. It was meant to help improve their morale. No sooner was my back turned than he turned it into a brawl!"

"And since they were fighting over me, it's my fault?" The ice in the woman's tone had been melted by pent-up anger. Surprised at her tone, Jackson just stared into her face.

"I've known Jack Gentleman for a long time, captain. He's dangerous, maybe crazy. I'm glad Steve Bard was there to get him off me!"

"I'm afraid you don't understand, Miss Lane. If I allow Bard to fight on this post and go unpunished, my men might well think they can do the same. Go wild." He shook his head, frowning, wondering how best to explain. Maybe the man at West Point had been right. Fighting Indians was better than this!

"What are you going to do to him?" Lane demanded to know.

"I intend to initiate the necessary steps to have Bard fired as a civilian scout. Charge him with violation of the rules of good order and discipline. He'll never work for the United States army again!"

Lane started to protest, but he went on. "It's one of those things. I don't suppose a woman should be expected to understand the need for strict discipline. I'll be most happy when this Indian scare is ended and you settlers can go back to your homes."

Lane Lester was on the point of telling him she had no home. The only thing she owned at this point was several decks of cards, a team of horses, a wagon and the few possessions that were in it. Her attention was suddenly diverted by a cry from a sentry at the gate.

"Two riders! Comin' fast! One of 'em looks like an Injun!"

Chapter Eighteen

Captain Jackson reacted, looking about uncertainly as he heard the cry of the sentry.

He had fought his share of Indians during nearly a decade in the West, but he had always been following orders. He had been hoping to get through this interim period of command without any major incidents. It didn't appear the gods who govern the military mortals were going to be of any help.

Between the wagons making up the refugee camp, the officer quickly spotted several men armed with scythes that were carried with the oak handles over their shoulders. The handles were crude, twisted creations, but as the group marched toward the gate, they were almost military in their appearance. Most, Jackson knew, had been in the war on one side or the other, but now they were only intent on cutting hay for their work teams and saddle horses that had been confined to one of the cavalry's corrals. This harvesting of feed had become a morning practice, since the soldiers bare-ly managed to cut and store enough hay for their own mounts, most of which were kept in the stables. Normally, the high grass was scythed down and allowed to dry during the day. In late afternoon, it was loaded on wagons and brought into the fort before the evening dew could ruin it. At night, it was covered with sections of tent canvas against dew and rain.

Standing there, Jackson suddenly found himself wondering why he was staring at a batch of settlers, instead of worrying about the two mounted men headed for his fort. The gate was being swung open as he noted that Lane Lester was staring in that direction, anticipating the entry of the reported horsemen.

"Miss Lester, please go and tell those men they can't cut hay right now. It may not be safe for them," the officer ordered. "Not until we know what's going on here!"

Lane glanced at him, surprised at his tone. He sounded as though he was speaking to one of his privates. In spite of a sudden rush of resentment, she stalked quickly to the edge of the encampment to face a large, bearded man who headed up the hay-cutting contingent.

Jackson watched her for a moment, then strode toward the open gate. He could hear the thunder of approaching hooves.

He dreaded what he was going to learn, for he was pretty certain as to the identity of the two riders. For years, the captain had been hiding his self-felt inadequacies behind a rigid show of what he considered professionalism. He had come to realize somewhere along the way that his problem was his name, but knowing the truth and simply accepting it as a matter of life being life was something he had yet to learn to handle.

Half a mile behind the fleeing bare-chested Bard and the journalist, Jud Ransom held up his hand and pulled his horse to a halt. Behind him, nearly two dozen hard-cases also drew rein.

"We almost got 'em!" one rider complained. Ransom shook his head, turning his horse to face his men.

"They've got forty soldiers in there not to mention th' civilians. We don't have th' strength to ride in now." He addressed the rider who had voiced his disappointment. "They'll prob'ly send out a rider to find those other two cavalry troops and bring them in."

Ransom nodded to indicate the heavy caliber rifle the grizzled man held across his saddle. The weapon was a Sharps .50 caliber instrument that its grizzled owner had used in killing hordes of buffalo for their hides. With the buffalo all but gone, the man felt he had been lucky to find employment of sorts with the rancher's band of ruffians.

"Seth, I want you to unlimber that rifle. When a rider comes out that gate, kill him. We can't let him or anyone else warn th' rest of th' cavalry."

He paused to glance about, concentrating on a tree line they had ridden through in their pursuit of Bard and Blade.

"Th' rest of you get back there in them trees. Stay hid 'til I come back with Long Arm and his warriors. We'll have proper strength then to attack. Th' damned Indians want them rifles bad."

As Ransom reined his horse to ride away toward the spot where he was supposed to meet the Indian and his band of renegades, the other riders paused for a moment to watch him. Then, on signal from the man called Seth, they all turned their horses and rode back to the thicket, where most of them dismounted to stretch and grumble about the way things were going. Some of them didn't think they needed a "bunch of redskins to take on the blue bellies!" as one rider put it. There was mixed agreement on that score.

Inside the fort, Jim Blade had dismounted and was helping Bard slide from his saddle.

"What's this all about, Mr. Blade!" Captain Jackson demanded. The journalist turned to glare at him.

"This man's hurt. Been tortured. Get your doctor."

"Dr. Robbins is out with the troops," the officer declared. He stared at the raw burn on Bard's chest, then glanced about as though hoping to conjure up a surgeon. Soldiers and settlers were gathering there near the gate, wanting to know what was going on.

It had been Jackson's decision to send the doctor and his horse-drawn ambulance—actually a canvas-covered spring wagon—with one of the troops of cavalry.

The doctor was a used-up old man, who was sloven in his personal ways and, Jackson felt, equally inept in his practice of medicine. Luckily, about all the old man was asked to do was patch up an occasional bullet wound or cut an arrowhead out of one of the troopers from time to time.

In spite of his dislike for the man, Jackson also feared him. The doctor and the colonel had served together in the War Between the States. In fact, it was rumored that the colonel had been instrumental in getting the doctor, Hiram Slade, his contract to serve as the civilian surgeon for Fort Wingate. The captain knew the two men were chess-playing friends and often spent long evenings together. The captain was certain a lot of information the colonel would not hear through normal channels was passed during those contests.

Bard straightened, reaching up to grab his saddle horn for support, leaning against the lathered horse. Lane had taken one look at the inflamed, seeping wound on his chest and had run toward her wagon.

"It's Ransom," the scout announced, addressing the cavalry officer. His tone was pained and he grimaced with the effort of simply breathing, let alone talking. "He's found gold somewhere on Massacre Mountain and he don't want homesteaders takin' over the land." The scout formed his words carefully, staring at Jackson, as he spoke. "His bunch and the Indians'll slaughter everyone here to keep them away!"

"That's ridiculous!" the soldier declared. "Jud Ransom's a respected rancher. He's done much to settle this country!"

"He's organized Long Arm's renegades and they're going to attack this fort," Blade stated, glaring at the soldier. "Captain, you'd damned well better get ready to defend this place or your scalp'll most likely be hanging from some brave's lance before this time tomorrow!"

Sergeant Major Keene had pushed his way to the front of the crowd. He also was glaring at the captain. "It makes sense, captain, but Troop D is due back here today. We'd best send a rider to bring them boys ridin' in here on th' double!"

Keene looked at Bard. "How many men's Ransom got, Steve?" The scout shook his head, still hanging onto the saddle.

"I don't know. At least twenty professionals. Some look to be former soldiers. Some're just gunfighters. There may be more, but it's the Navajos we've gotta worry more about. There'll be a batch of them."

"At least Jack Gentleman's dead," Blade put in. "Steve killed him."

Lane Lester paused in her efforts to treat Bard's wound and looked up at him. His eyes were on her as he offered a quiet nod. She was aware that he was letting her know she wouldn't be bothered any more. Not by Jud Ransom's gun hawk, at least. The renegade Indians could be another matter.

"Send a dispatch rider, sergeant major. Get him on the way immediately." Jackson respected the reasoning of the old soldier. Keene, he knew, had been fighting Indians when the officer was in knee pants.

The sergeant major cast the officer a somewhat sloppy salute, a possible indication that he had little use for sloppi-ly presented command decisions. He strode away, showing unusual agility for his age as Lane Lester shoved through the crowd. She carried a clean white sheet, a bottle containing some kind of salve and a pair of scissors in one hand. Under her other arm, she had a rolled buckskin jacket. She shoved the jacket toward Jim Blade, who took it and shook it out. It was almost new and a lot cleaner than the jacket stripped from Bard in Ransom's office. Lane turned to hand the cutting tool and the folded sheet to one of the women settlers who had been watching.

"Here! Cut up some bandages. They have to be big enough to go around his body!"

The elderly woman, face shadowed by a giant sunbonnet, hesitated for an instant, uncertain, then offered a nod and went about the assigned chore. Lane turned to use a clean, lace-edged handkerchief she had brought to dab the burned area on Bard's chest with the salve.

The scout grimaced in pain at the treatment and at one point a groan escaped his lips, but Lane ignored it, coating the burn heavily with the jelly-like concoction. From the appearance of the bottle in which it was stored, it looked like a frontier remedy rather than something that had come from a pharmacist.

"What else can you tell me?" Jackson wanted to know, addressing Blade, who still hung onto Bard with one hand, supporting him, while the other clutched the jacket Lane had brought.

"We sneaked up on Ransom's place. Steve went in close enough to hear what was being said. He got caught and they used a lighted torch on him." He hesitated waiting for his words to soak in before he added, "They wanted to know how many of the new '73 Winchesters you've got and where they're stored."

From somewhere nearby, Sergeant Major Keene shouted, "Rider comin' out. Move it!"

As a young corporal loped past the gathering, the gate was hurriedly thrown open by the sentry. The minute he was outside the perimeter, the gate was swung closed. Lane had finished bandaging Bard's burn and took the buckskin jacket from Blade. She draped it over Bard's shoulders.

"This belonged to my brother," she told the scout. "He was a little heavier than you, but at least it'll keep you covered up." Bard managed to cast her a weak smile.

"Alright, people, we have to get ready to defend this fort 'til our other troops can get here!" Jackson had turned to survey the crowd of civilians who were wondering what was happening. At least, he reminded himself, what lay immediately ahead was something he knew how to handle. Fort defense had been drilled into him over the years of his service.

"You men get your firearms and I'll put each of you with one of my soldiers to form a team. One man shoots while the other reloads!"

The civilians moved about uncertainly for a moment. Then they saw that members of the fort's cadre already were mounting ladders and taking their places on elevated walkways from which they could fire down on attackers. All movement was halted suddenly as the roar of a heavy-caliber rifle roared a long way off. It was followed instantly by a fusillade from weapons of lesser caliber.

"Damn!" Jackson muttered under his breath. He knew what the sound meant. His messenger was dead. Judging from the stark expressions on those closest to him, each one of them also knew what those gunshots meant.

Chapter Nineteen

As Jesse James heard the roar of the Sharps buffalo gun
followed by the clatter of shots from arms of smaller caliber,
he pulled up his horse and raised his hand in signal. Behind
him, the other three men came to a halt. Jeb Smith was
mounted behind Clell Miller and Frank James was leading
the lame horse.

"Sounded like a Sharps," Jesse ventured. They had just
ridden into a gully and had started up the other side, when
they had been stopped by the fusillade of firing. Frank led
the limping mount up to stop beside his brother.

"Sounded like them was all rifle shots," he added. "Looks
like maybe Jud Ransom's started his own private little war."

Both Clell and Jeb were heavy men, each weighing close
to two hundred pounds, and the horse on which both were
mounted was gasping noisily, flanks heaving at the extra
exertion required to carry the two of them.

Smith slid off the horse over its rump and adjusted his
gun belt, which had crept up under his ribs during his
uncomfortable ride. He stood beside Clell's horse as he eyed
the James brothers, wondering what was happening.

Before they had ridden into the gully, they had been able to see the fort less than a mile away. It had been decided as they were breaking camp earlier that the best course of action was to ride back to the military installation and get the duty blacksmith to put a new shoe on the lame horse. Given a day of rest after the shoeing at the fort, the animal should be ready to ride. Frank had pointed out that they had a lot of rough country ahead.

It wouldn't hurt to have the military blacksmith check the shoes on all their horses. Making about twelve dollars a month, as he did, the soldier should be more than happy to accept a couple of bucks for his work. At least that had been the plan until the firing had started so close by.

Clell Mill and Jeb had been working at Jesse's small ranch in West Texas, when Frank James had arrived to announce that the Pinkerton detectives hired by the railroads and bankers were on their trail. The brothers had not been seen or heard from in more than six months at the time of Frank's arrival at the Texas ranch. He had bought a farm in Tennessee and had gone pretty much respectable until word came to him that the Pinks were in town, looking for him and Jesse.

With Miller and Smith, the brothers had ridden away from the Texas ranch only hours after Jesse had handed the deed to a neighboring rancher, telling the surprised man that he had an emergency. The neighbor could pay him what the place was worth later.

The first thought had been to ride to a railroad and board a train headed for the West Coast, putting them as far from the Pinkertons as possible. It had become apparent that the Texas railroads were being watched closely. Instead, the four of them had headed west into New Mexico.

The James brothers' mother had long been after them to go to California and find the grave of their father, who had gone west during the Gold Rush of 1849. A minister, he had insisted God would help him find gold. God may have had little to do with it, but word had come back that the Reverend James had died of pneumonia in the vicinity of Marysville, California, and had been buried there. This looked like a good time for the brothers to search for the grave.

Strangers in the New Mexico country, they had overridden their goal, which was Santa Fe. From there, they could catch a train to Denver, then take another westward to California. They had been seeking help with maps and whatever information the officers at Fort Wingate could offer, when they had run into the man who now called himself Jud Ransom.

During their time with Ransom's outlaw crew, they found that they were going to have to backtrack and ride north to reach Santa Fe. They were told it was probably a five-day ride, but the trail was well-marked because most of the supplies for the fort came from that city to the north.

As they hunkered in the dry-bottomed coulee, each of the men was interested primarily in getting the horse reshod so they could be on their way. The sound of the rifle shots left each man wondering whether they'd ever reach Santa Fe.

"Wait!" Jesse ordered, not looking at the others. His eyes were on the rim of the gully.

The Missourian swung down from his mount and handed the reins to his brother, then began to scramble up the steep embankment. Close to the top, he dropped to his knees to remove his broad-brimmed hat and peer over the edge of the depression.

"One dead soldier and a hurt horse," he reported. "I don't see nothin' else."

Then he stiffened. There was movement in the thicket not far from the gully.

"There's a whole pack of people in them woods over there," he announced, ducking beneath the top edge of the ravine to avoid being seen. "A coupla them even look downright familiar."

"See Ransom?" Frank wanted to know. Jesse shook his head.

"No, but they're all his men. He's no doubt there somewheres amongst them."

"What're we gonna do?" Clell wanted to know. They all realized something had to be done about getting the lame horse shod or they would have to come up with another horse.

"For right now, we're just gonna sit here and see what happens," Jesse decided. "Might as well get down and stretch some. Save th' horses."

Frank slowly swung down from his mount, offering a grimace of pain.

"What's th' matter, Frank? You just gettin' old?" Jesse asked with the suggestion of a grin.

"Too damned old to be sleepin' on th' ground," the brother declared. "Tends to stiffen a man up."

Less than a hundred yards away, hidden in the thicket, Seth Muldoon clutched his .50 caliber Sharps and eyed what had been a human being who was now a shapeless lump lying in the grass. The man's uniform had been turned into nothing more than a mess of bloody blue rags, a result of the fusillade from the twenty or so outlaws.

One of the bullets had struck the dead rider's horse in the upper leg and it was standing thirty feet from the body. The animal knew it was hurt, but attempted to take a tentative step. The leg crumpled beneath the gelding and it fell. The horse lay still for a moment, then raised its head and attempted to struggle to its feet.

Seth Muldoon leveled his .50 caliber Sharps buffalo gun,

aligned the sights and squeezed the trigger with practiced gentleness. The big bullet took the horse in the head. The animal was as dead as its rider before its bulk hit the ground. The impact of the animal's weight threw up a little puff of dust that dissipated on the early morning breeze.

"You're wastin' ammo!" one of the outlaws declared. "It wasn't nothin' but a horse!"

Muldoon cast the scroungy-looking outlaw a solitary glance as he loaded another round into the rifle's chamber.

"I like horses better'n I like a lotta people," the old buffa-lo hunter declared.

The outlaw offered a grimace and turned away. The narrow-eyed glance Muldoon had cast him suggested noth-ing more should be said about the shot or the horse.

"Damned *cimarron*," the outlaw muttered under his breath as he stared at the fort. The term, borrowed from the Spanish, had come to mean a loner in the Southwest.

In Jackson's office, the captain was standing behind his desk, possibly a subconscious means of separating himself from the pair who stood before him. He scowled at Steve Bard, who was seated across from him. Jim Blade occupied the other chair.

"I should have known you were up to something devious," Jackson charged, glaring at Bard. The scout, however, seemed unperturbed by the accusation, simply matching the officer's scowl.

"You'd do best to be gettin' ready for that attack instead of talkin', captain."

"My men are forming up now. We'll be riding out within the hour for that trail crossing you mentioned."

Bard, staring at the officer, shook his head slowly. "I may be short on tactical trainin', but don't you stay inside a fort to defend it?"

"If we surprise the Indians, they'll never get to the fort. We can wipe them out—at least, send them packing—and be back here before they know we're around," Jackson insisted. Bard rose abruptly from his chair to glare at, the officer.

"It won't work!"

"A general I once served under proved that the best defense is a good offense. U.S. Grant proved it to you and your General Lee!"

There was a forceful note in Jackson's tone that caused Bard's eyes to narrow dangerously. When he spoke, however, his tone was soft, seeming to carry a note of pity.

"And your General Grant never fought Indians, captain!"

Jackson ignored the scout, turning to Blade, his tone crisp and businesslike.

"Mr. Blade, I'm leaving a small garrison detachment here. I'm putting you in charge of the settlers. If you should be attacked, you are to work with my men in defending the fort. Is that understood?"

Blade glanced at Bard, saw the tight-jawed expression on his face, then looked up at the officer. "I'm a civilian, captain."

"But you were a soldier once. There's one Gatling gun in the armory, but we won't take it. We'll be moving too fast for it to keep up. Use it here!"

Before either man could comment, Jackson rounded his desk and, stiff-backed, strode to the door, slamming it behind him, Blade looked at Bard.

"What's going to happen, Steve?"

Bard's tone was flat, seemingly devoid of emotion. "A massacre, if that idiot has his way!"

The scout turned toward the door, squaring his shoulders. The effort brought a grimace to his lips and a hand went to the buckskin jacket in the area that covered his bandaged burn.

"Where're you going?" Blade wanted to know.

"To try to keep that damned fool from killin' off his troops!"

As Bard opened the door, he found Lane Lester standing before it, her hand raised as though to knock. Bard cast her a look of surprise. There was a note of uncertainty in the woman's voice as she spoke.

"Can I see you for a moment?" she wanted to know. Blade had risen and moved to the door. He paused behind Bard, who blocked his way.

"If you'll move, Steve, I'll go see about that Gatling gun."

Bard stepped aside, still looking down at Lane, his expression one of puzzlement.

She reached out to finger the ragged fringe on the buckskin jacket Bard wore over his bandage.

"I think my brother'd be proud to see you wearing it," she said quietly. Her eyes were on the fringe rather than Bard's face. He hunched his shoulders as though checking the fit of the jacket.

"Seems to fit fine. I thank you for th' loan."

Lane's gaze rose to inspect his face. "Do you have to be so formal, Steve?"

"I'd best get movin'," the scout announced, starting to step past her. She tightened her hand on the leather fringe.

"I came to kiss you for luck, Steve." Her voice was soft, carrying a note of want. The scout halted in mid-stride, looking down at her, then reaching up to grasp a shoulder in each hand. He bent to kiss her and an arm went around his neck. Several seconds passed before he reached up to pull the arm away and stare into her eyes, his gaze even more puzzled than before. She smiled at him, voice soft.

"Thanks, Steve."

"Right now, we're needin' all the luck we can gather!"

Bard heaved a sigh, started to say more, but simply nodded and turned to stride away toward the stables from which uniformed troops already were leading out their saddled mounts. Lane Lester was still smiling as she looked after him. She couldn't see his face nor the trace of a smile he wore.

Chapter Twenty

Seth Muldoon was disturbed. The wind was coming into the grove of trees from the direction of the fort and on the increasingly strong breeze, he could hear the crying of a child. He glared toward the fort for a long moment, then rose from where he had been hunkered. He grabbed up his rifle and began to walk farther into the grove where the band's horses had been tied.

"Where you goin', Seth?" one of the outlaws wanted to know. The old buffalo hunter paused long enough to jerk his head in the direction of the child's cries.

"There's kids in that fort. I ain't killin' no kids."

"You've been takin' Ransom's pay. You cain't go coyotin' outa here now. We'll be launchin' th' attack soon as them redskins show up."

Muldoon shook his head. "He don't pay me 'nough to be killin' young'uns." The grizzled old timer turned and approached his gray mare, untying her as the other man watched, glowering. Without a backward glance, the old hunter mounted the animal and looked for the closest way out of the growth of trees. There looked to be a coulee—

some kind of drainage of some sort, at least—a hundred yards or so away. He figured that if he could make it that far, he would be able to get clear without the soldiers in the fort getting a good shot at him.

With the old Sharps balanced across his saddle, Muldoon spurred his way out of the trees, headed for the depression that would offer him and his mount protective cover. Little did he know that four men in need of a horse were hidden in that draw. Jesse James, looking quickly over the lip of the ravine, watched the rider approaching at a gallop.

"Here comes your horse, Jeb," the train robber muttered, unholstering his six-gun.

But before Jesse could align the handgun's crude sights on the approaching rider there sounded a rifle shot, coming from the grove of trees out of which the man had just ridden. The old man lurched forward, dropping his rifle, then loose-limbed, tumbled headfirst out of the saddle.

The horse, spooked at the fire and loss of her rider, continued straight ahead and Jesse James was forced to roll out of the way to keep clear of the driving hooves, as the animal plunged into the coulee. Several more shots from the tree line thunked into the old buffalo hunter's body. There was no movement from what obviously had become a corpse.

A desperate Jeb Smith was able to grab the horse's bridle, as the wild-eyed animal lurched into the bottom of the draw. The young outlaw was able to wrestle the mare to a halt, the animal snorting and shivering with fright. The train robber began to speak to her with reassuring softness, rubbing the mare's neck in a practiced effort to calm her.

"Looks like we can ride outa here now," he observed, glancing to where Jesse, now standing with his six-gun in one hand, was trying to brush the dust from his clothing.

"Not just yet," Jesse James muttered, glancing toward the upper edge of the ravine once more. "Looks like Jud

Ransom don't care who he shoots. He figgers if you ain't with him, you're for sure against him. And we ain't with him!"

Jesse stepped to his own mount and drew the Winchester rifle from its scabbard. There was a moment's hesitation before the others began to arm themselves with long guns.

The rifle shots had been heard inside the stockade, where Steve Bard, Captain Jackson, Sergeant Major Seth Keene and Jim Blade were gathered about a bulky brass creation known as the Gatling gun. The officer raised his eyes to look up at one of the military sentries positioned on an elevated rampart that allowed him to see over the twelve-foot barricade fence.

"What was that?" the captain wanted to know.

"A man rode outa them trees an' somebody shot him," came the puzzled reply. "Looked like he was headed away."

Jackson pondered for a second, then turned back to the Gatling gun. Not far away, half a dozen male civilians had gathered, curious about the strange weapon. From behind them, Lane Lester and several other women watched the preparations being made. It was likely none of them had ever seen such an instrument of war.

Jackson cast a glance at Blade. "You know anything about one of these guns, Mr. Blade?"

Jim Blade offered a tight nod. "A little. I had a chance to fire one during the Battle of Petersburg in Sixty-four. But that was all more than ten years ago."

"The gun hasn't changed. You and the sergeant major will operate this gun." The officer turned to look at the gathering of civilians, "Any of you know anything about the Gatling?"

There were no volunteers, although several men rocked on their heels uncomfortably, frustrated by ignorance perhaps. Jackson pointed to a pair of young men standing together.

"We need the pair of you to help with the loading." As the officer was speaking, several uniformed soldiers were lugging lengthy magazines from the armory, stacking them beside the gun, which had been positioned just inside the fort's main gate.

The captain glanced at his senior enlisted man. "Sergeant major, you'll be the gunner and Mr. Blade can spot targets for you."

"Just what's your plan, captain?" Bard wanted to know. "There are at least twenty hard-cases with rifles out there in them woods. They're just waitin' for the Navajos to join up."

Jackson offered a tight nod. "I understand that, Steve. When my troop rides out, we will be at full gallop. I want all of them firing into those trees as they ride. I also want Blade and Sergeant Major Keene to lay down a blanket of fire on those people hidden in there."

He offered a sigh as he allowed his words to sink in. "Maybe if we can make them keep their heads down, they'll be too busy to shoot back."

Bard considered the plan for a moment, then nodded. He glanced at the Gatling gun, where Blade and Keene were instructing the two young civilians in the method of loading the long magazines into the top of the brass mechanism.

The Gatling gun, invented by a medical doctor, one Richard Jordan Gatling, had been patented in 1862 and saw limited service during the Civil War on the Union side. Originally, it fired a .58 caliber bullet that was powered by a paper cartridge. Before the War Between the States ended, Gatling had introduced his Model 1865 gun, which fired rimfire copper-cased cartridges at a sustained rate of fire of up to six hundred rounds per minute!

During the earlier days of the war, the Union army had rejected the design as too complicated, but a dozen of the guns had been purchased at $1,000 each by Major General Benjamin F. Butler. It was these guns that had been used in a major battle near Petersburg, Virginia, where Blade had taken part. The Army had taken to the improved model and Gatling guns were issued to frontier units throughout the west after hostilities ended.

Gatling's improved design featured six barrels and was mounted on a pair of iron-rimmed oak wheels, so it could be transported to the field by a team of horses. The odd-looking shooting machine was powered by a hand-crank that turned the barrels and caused the gun to be fired through all of the six barrels with each turn. After each cartridge was fired, the continuing action drew back the lock to drop the spent cartridge case to the ground, instantly loading a fresh round into the chamber. Each barrel had its own firing mechanism that resulted in a simultaneous working of locks, barrels, carrier and breech.

"How many of these guns've you got?" Blade asked the sergeant major as the two of them worked with the gun, inserting the first lengthy magazine through the port in the top of the mechanism.

"Three, but the other two're on patrol with the troops," the old soldier replied. He had removed his uniform blouse and his issue long johns, which were already darkening with perspiration.

The veteran Indian fighter and the journalist worked at aligning the barrel of the gun so it would be pointed at the grove when the gate was opened, while Bard and the captain joined the mounted troop that was aligned in the fort's street. Blade, mounting his own horse, listened closely to the order that explained how the cavalrymen would go through the gate at a full gallop, each rider bearing to the left to stay clear of the muzzle of the Gatling gun that would be blasting away with supporting fire.

The captain was aware that Bard had been listening to the orders as he rode up to position his mount on the officer's flank. Jackson turned to cast him a glance.

"Anything to add, Mr. Bard?"

"You've said it all. Let's go find Long Arm and his bunch!"

On signal from the officer, the assigned sentry swung the gate open quickly. No sooner was the grove of trees visible than Sergeant Major Keene began to turn the gun's operating crank. The big .58 caliber bullets began to stream toward the wooded area.

In the same moment, Captain Jackson raised his arm and brought it down in a slashing motion, shouting at the same time. He drove his spurs into the flank of his mount and it bounded forward, startled at what was happening. Bard's horse was a few yards behind him.

There was firing from the thicket of trees, but at Blade's direction, the gunner turned the barrel a bit and continued to crank the gun. As a magazine was emptied, one of the younger men jerked it out of the loading port and the other quickly jammed a fresh one in place.

Two cavalrymen fell from their saddles during the initial rush, one of them obviously dead, the other wounded. The gate sentry tossed his rifle aside, then hunched low, running a dozen yards into the open to grab the wounded man by the heels and drag him back within the bounds of the stockade. Bullets from the thicket kicked up the dust around him.

The string of mounted horsemen, Jackson and Bard in the lead, streamed past the grove, firing their handguns into the thicket as they passed. They could hear screams of pain and curses of frustration from the outlaws hidden there. It was obvious the fire from the string of cavalrymen, supplemented by that of the big-bore Gatling gun, was doing damage.

Clutching a torn-up sheet, Lane Lester was followed by another woman, as they ran behind the Gatling gun and dropped to their knees beside the wounded cavalryman, who had been shot in the leg. Both women seemed to ignore the firing as they dragged the man farther.

From their vantage point in the shallow ravine, Jesse and the others were watching the action. They had been surprised when the gate had suddenly opened and the automatic weapon had begun pouring fire into the wooded area.

"That Yankee captain knows what he's doin'," Frank James muttered.

"We might as well help out," Jesse suggested. He had his rifle in hand and leveled it across the top of the ravine, seeking a target in the woods.

"You're really gonna side them blue bellies, Jesse?" Clell Miller wanted to know. There was a strong note of disapproval in his tone.

"I ain't sidin' nobody. I'm just helpin' to kill Jud Ransom's dreams of an empire!" Jesse declared as he found a target and triggered the rifle. The figure dropped, but he couldn't tell whether he had scored a hit or this gunman had simply taken cover after being shot at from an unexpected quarter.

Moments later, the other three men were lined up at the top of the ditch, looking for targets and firing at will. The rapid fire from the Gatling gun continued to smash into the underbrush, some of the bullets cutting down small trees. There also were the screams of wounded horses that had been hidden there.

It wasn't long before riders began to appear, spurring their way out of the grove. There was no concerted effort, no chosen direction. Each of the riders was simply seeking escape. The Gatling gun continued to tear at the wooded cover, soldiers and civilian marksmen on the fort's ramparts, putting down several of the escaping horsemen.

Suddenly the firing stopped. There was a deathly silence broken after a moment by the sounds of a crying child somewhere within the confines of the fort. Jesse James backed down from the top of the ravine's wall and jammed his rifle into its scabbard.

"Let's get mounted up," he suggested, really an order. "I reckon we can get along to California now."

Chapter Twenty-One

Long Arm had rounded up his band of sixty-odd Navajo reservation jumpers. Several were approaching middle age as was their leader. One of these older men even wore the familiar hat and blue blouse marked with the insignia of a cavalry lieutenant. Both no doubt had been taken during an earlier raid. Most of the Navajos, however, were young warriors who may have campaigned against other tribes, stealing horses and looting their camps, but none had faced the U.S. Cavalry head-on.

Long Arm's anger was not without reason. The reservation system was totally corrupt. The cattle the tribe was supposed to get for food invariably came up short in number. The full allotment had been paid for, but someone was skimming off the money. At one point, the U.S. Government had attempted to introduce cattle raising. Five hundred brood cows and several bulls were supposed to be driven to the reservation. What arrived were steers, impossible for breeding. The Navajos had simply slaughtered the steers and eaten them. When the powers in Washington heard of this, they said the Navajos were irresponsible.

162

Long Arm, of course, was not familiar with the workings of the graft involved. He simply knew that his people were often hungry.

Some of these younger men had dismounted from their ponies, but most sat their mounts, a number clutching badly used single-shot rifles. Others were armed with an array of bows, arrows and feather-decorated lances.

All of the Indians had heard the distant sounds of gunfire and were puzzled, some of them even nervous, wondering what those sounds of battle could mean. There were troubled mutterings among the older warriors, but Long Arm, sitting apart from them on his horse, ignored what was being discussed. His face was dark with anger.

Ransom had called their meeting for dawn. The white-eye rancher was supposed to be here with his men. He was more than an hour late. The renegade leader never before had heard the sounds of a firing Gatling gun and at this distance of several miles, it sounded to him like the rattling of a diamondback rattler; a sound of death!

Behind his frown, Long Arm was pondering the wisdom of committing himself and his band of renegades to the rancher. The distant gunfire suddenly had halted but it left him wondering. It might be better for his band to drift back into the hills and wait for another day to attack the fort for its rifles.

Ransom and his men had tortured the captured scout for information concerning the new rifles, but the sounds of gunfire would suggest the man named Bard had not been caught before he reached the fort. If so, their element of surprise would be gone. With full daylight, there would be no sneaking through the fort's open gates.

The Indian was on the point of signaling his warriors that they were done with waiting, when he saw Ransom and another rider approaching along the trail that was flanked on each side by rocky cliffs. Long Arm issued a gutteral order for his men to wait, while he heeled his pony forward at a walk to meet the rancher and the man riding with him.

As Ransom and the other man approached at a lope, the rancher raised his hand in the Indian signal of friendship. Long Arm simply sat his pony, staring, wondering where the rest of Ransom's gunmen might be.

Ransom recognized the fact that the Indian was concerned, even angry. The rider with him had been one of Gentleman's recent hirings and he didn't even know the man's name beyond the fact that the late Jack Gentleman had called him Sid.

The man had been punishing his horse, riding hard, when he had come up with Ransom. The distant sounds of firing had come to a halt, but the rancher had more than an inkling as to what had happened. The rapid-fire sounds of the Gatling gun had come as an unexpected surprise. He hadn't known the fort was armed with such deadly firepower. That was the sort of information Kalispell Kane was supposed to have reported. He had been killed before he could pass on the information.

The fleeing rider recognized Ransom and both men drew up their horses almost within sight of the crossroads where the Navajos were supposed to be waiting.

"You bringin' me a message?" Ransom wanted to know, although he knew better. The man's wild-eyed appearance and the way he kept looking over his back trail were a giveaway. He was definitely on the run!

"I'm getting outa this country," the man told him. "Them soljer's killed near all of us!"

"The cavalry troop? Where's it?"

Sid jerked his head to the rear. "They're formed up back there somewheres, ridin' this way."

"I heard a Gatling gun. Do they have one with them?" Ransom questioned, tone harsh.

Sid hesitated. It took him an instant to realize Ransom was talking about the fast-firing gun that had cut down part of the grove's trees, not to mention many of his companions. He shook his head.

"Don't think so," he declared. "I didn't see nothin' but horse soljers come outa the fort."

"It's dangerous out here, Sid. You'd better ride along with me." Ransom made it sound like an order. "If the cavalry doesn't get you, the Indians probably will, if you're ridin' alone!"

As they rode down the trail, neither man realized that they had been seen. On a cliff above them, Jeb Smith sat behind a boulder, his rifle resting across the big rock. Perhaps thirty yards behind him, hidden in a depression, Frank James was brewing coffee and trying to fry strips of bacon over a small dry-wood fire. It had been necessary to cut the mold off the slab of meat before slicing thick pieces.

They had been lucky enough to spot a small stream and had ridden into the rocks to find its source. There they had filled their canteens before starting the fire for coffee. The coffee and slab of bacon was the full extent of their food and they had decided to head for Fort Defiance, thirty miles away, where they could get supplies.

Fort Defiance, they had learned while at Ransom's headquarters, was no longer a working military establishment. Instead, it had become the seat of administration for the Navajo Reservation. It was to this headquarters that the Navajos came each month to collect their rations of beef, flour and beans, but Frank James felt they could stock up there on supplies for their own ride.

From Fort Defiance, they could move eastward in what

was judged to be a five-day ride to Santa Fe and the railroad. With luck, the Pinkerton detectives wouldn't have tracked them this far west. Originally, they had considered riding all the way to the Pacific Coast, but tales from some of Gentleman's men as to what could befall one in the heat and seemingly endless wastelands of the Mojave Desert had caused them to rethink their route to Marysville.

"I'll be more'n happy to get shut of this country," Frank James groused, as he checked the coffee pot.

"When we get to Santa Fe, we'd best split up. Not all go on th' same train. You and me'll wait till th' next day," Jesse announced. Frank had no chance to comment on the plan.

"Jesse, you'd best come look at this!" Jeb had turned away from his post and cupped his hands around his mouth megaphone-fashion to call in a low voice.

Jesse James, who had been sitting close to the fire, watching hungrily as the bacon cooked, spitted on thin green branches, looked up, frowning. He didn't really want to move. He was enjoying just the smell of food.

However, he saw the anxious expression on the young gang member's face and heaved himself to his feet, ambling toward the boulder that overlooked the trail. A moment later, he was lying beside Jeb Smith, watching the approach by Jud Ransom and the other rider. Looking in the other direction, he could see Long Arm walking his horse to meet the rancher. Beyond the Indian was a jutting extension in the cliff's rock face that voided the chance to see what lay beyond.

"What do you make of it?" Smith wanted to know, glancing at his leader. Jesse, scowling, shook his head.

"Trouble!" was Jesse's hissed evaluation. He turned his head to glance to the rear, where Frank was seated. The older brother was watching as Jesse rose abruptly and waved at him. Frank rose quickly and stalked over to face Jesse. "What's up?"

"Ransom's ridin' in to meet an Indian looks like. There may be more of them 'round th' bend."

Frank stared at him for a moment. "Hope not. That's the trail to Fort Defiance. We gotta go that way!"

Without comment, Jesse turned and skittered along the cliff, staying well back from the edge. Frank followed him at a somewhat slower pace. When he had gone perhaps sixty yards or so, Jesse edged up to the cliff's edge and looked over. One look, and he jerked his head back.

Frank, twenty yards away, was about to speak, when Jesse rolled on his back and raised a finger to his lips, indicating a need for silence. Frank nodded his understanding and moved along the cliff until he was able to lie down next to his brother.

"What'd you see? What's down there?"

"A whole passel of Indians," Jesse told him. "Take a look."

Frank James crept forward to join his brother, both of them on their bellies and looking over the rim of the canyon. Looking down from the ragged edge, they could see the band of warriors on one side, the two horsemen and Long Arm on the other side.

"What're we gonna do, Jesse?"

Jesse James thought about it for a moment, then offered a grimace. "I want to take out Ransom. People like him deserve to die, but we don't want Indians all over us." He hesitated before deciding, "We wait. Get that fire out before some redskin smells it and comes to look."

On the floor of the canyon below, Long Arm had drawn up his horse, as Ransom and his underling reined to a halt facing him. The Indian was scowling.

"We attack fort? Get new rifles? Your men? Where are

they?" Long Arm wanted answers to all three questions. Ransom shook his head.

"Most of my men are already at the fort. You heard the firing."

"No firing now," came the guttural observation.

"They're savin' their bullets for th' full attack," Ransom lied.

"But the cavalry troop is head this way." Long Arm lifted his reins as though to turn his horse.

"Wait!" Ransom insisted, waving to the rugged cliffs. "Get your men hidden in them rocks and they can pick off the blue bellies as they come through th' canyon. We can wipe out th' whole troop." He paused, gauging the Indian's scowl, before adding, "Takin' the fort then'll be easy. No one there but a few civilians. Old men. Women. Children. Easy scalps!"

Long Arm considered the possibilities for a moment, then swung his mount about to look down the canyon, calling loudly in his native tongue. Several seconds later, the Indian wearing the cavalry hat and the blouse marked with the lieutenant's rank rode into view.

"Great!" Ransom exclaimed. "We can use him as a decoy!"

He explained quickly that the Indian in the partial uniform should ride to the mouth of the canyon. When he spotted the approaching cavalry troop, he should give them a wave, greeting them.

"Th' other two troops are due back at the fort late today or sometime tomorrow," Ransom explained. "That stupid captain will think he's about to join up with them. He'll ride right into our trap!"

Long Arm considered the plan for a moment, offered a tight nod of acceptance and swung to face the other Indian and explain in the Navajo language.

Jesse and Frank James watched as the Indian wearing the

items of cavalry uniform rode toward the mouth of the canyon. Long Arm, facing in the other direction, called loudly, his orders somewhat lengthy. In moments, Indians came out of the depths of the canyon and began to find hiding places in the rocks. Several had been left out of sight to tend the horses.

Lying on the cliff's edge, the James brothers were fully aware of what was taking place.

"Ol' Bloody Bill Quantrill could've learned some truly dirty tricks from Ransom," Jesse muttered beneath his breath.

"He did learn from Ransom," Frank pointed out. "That's what got him killed!"

Chapter Twenty-Two

Jud Ransom was worried, maybe even fearful, although he knew he couldn't allow Long Arm or any of his braves to know it. Nothing was going as he had spent so long in planning. He mouthed a silent curse. That damned meddling civilian scout had shot everything to Hell and gone!

He had been counting on his band of white renegades to back the Indians in the attack on the fort. Having Bard escape and trying to run him down before he could reach the fort and warn the cavalry had completely destroyed his time schedule. Now, it turned out, not only was Jack Gentleman gone, but most of the gang the gun hawk had controlled were either dead or lying wounded in the woods back there near the fort. Others had just fled.

He had always known his efforts were dangerous to his own welfare, but the lust for gold had made him less cautious. His Massacre Mountain holdings edged the Navajo Reservation and the gold was on Indian land. There had been earlier instances in which tribes had rebelled and the U.S. Government had taken away some of their reservation land as punishment. That was what he had planned for with his own plotting.

He had worked to make contacts in the Territorial Government who would be instrumental in what land would be taken from the Navajos for their insurrection. Once the land was free of reservation control, he could put some of his own men on important pieces of the property as homesteaders. A few had been Union veterans and held U.S. Army discharges.

In his safe at the office were similar honorable discharges that he had obtained by outright purchase from men who were down on their luck or others who had been slain in one manner or another.

He had been certain that if he could wipe out the civilians at the fort as well as the single troop of cavalry now on his trail, the wanted retribution against the Navajos would come about as planned.

He realized that anything he did now was far from his original plan. He was having to play it by ear. A lot depended upon when the two troops of cavalry were going to show up on their scheduled return to the fort.

"What're you aimin' to do, Mistah Ransom," the man named Sid wanted to know. He was leaning on his saddle horn, observing the preparations being made for battle.

"It's obvious," Ransom snarled at him. "We're going to destroy the cavalry troop!"

Sid shook his head. "Not me. I think I'll just ride on outa here before th' shootin' gets serious."

"Do you think you can get through this country on your own?"

Sid offered a shrug. "I don't know, but I'm for certain gonna try. My chances're less good against all them Yankee soljers!"

The outlaw said nothing more and reined his horse about to go return in the direction from which he had come. More than anything else, he wanted to get clear of the war-armed Navajos and the canyon. He had gone no more than twenty yards, when Ransom turned to nod at Long Arm, who had been watching the exchange.

"Kill him!" Ransom ordered. "No guns!"

Long Arm turned toward the nearest man now hidden in the rocky terrain. The Indian was armed with bow and arrows. The renegade leader shouted instructions in Navajo and the armed Indian rose from his place of concealment, drawing the bow. It was a shot of nearly fifty yards, but the arrow caught Sid squarely between the shoulder blades. The rider turned into a bundle of loose rags as he fell from his saddle. The flint arrowhead apparently had severed his spinal column.

At a signal from Long Arm, two young warriors rushed out of the rocks. One caught the dead man's horse and led it into a concealed position among the boulders, while the other grabbed Sid's body by the heels and dragged it into the rocks, where it would not be visible from the trail.

Atop the cliff, Jesse and Frank James were watching these happenings. They had not been surprised when Sid had decided to ride away. Neither were they surprised when Jud Ransom ordered the man slain. From their high perch, they could see a cloud of dust perhaps two miles away.

"Looks like th' horse soldiers are comin'," Frank ventured.

"We could end this whole thing right now, you know," Jesse muttered thoughtfully.

"How's that?"

"Take out Jud Ransom! This's all his doin'."

Frank James considered for a moment before he shook his head. "Then we'd be up to our bellies in mad Indians."

Jesse heaved a sigh, a sign that he couldn't argue with his brother's logic. He nodded to indicate the trail crossing below. "And that's th' trail to Fort Defiance. We're pretty much trapped 'til this is over."

Frustrated, Jesse James watched as Ransom dismounted and led his horse into the rocks, no longer offering an easy shot. Looking over the back trail, he could see that the cavalry unit, riding in column, had come to a stop.

At the head of the mounted column, Captain Jackson had signaled for the halt. He turned to glare at Steve Bard who had been riding beside him.

"This is a wild goose chase, Bard. No sign of even a single Indian all morning," the captain declared, trying hard to keep his observation from turning into an ungentlemanly snarl of frustration.

Bard didn't look at him. Instead, he was staring straight ahead to the mouth of the canyon. On the center of the canyon was where the two trails crossed, one leading to the reservation, the other to Massacre Mountain.

"'Bout now's when we should be worryin', captain. I've found most Indians tend to be where you don't see them." Bard's tone was noncommittal, but he stiffened in his saddle, squinting as he continued to stare. "Look up there, captain."

Jackson swiveled his gaze once more to the mouth of the canyon. What appeared to be a horse soldier was waving to them, beckoning them to ride toward him.

"Scout for one of the troops," Jackson announced, turning his head to shout, "Forward! Ho!"

"Hold up!" Bard called. "That's no cavalry horse!"

The cavalry captain either didn't hear his warning or simply ignored it. The officer spurred his horse forward and the column of cavalry began to follow. They had gone no more than fifty yards, when a rifle shot sounded and the Indian wearing the cavalry hat and blouse fell from his horse.

Suddenly, there was fire from a variety of rifles coming from the canyon. Several soldiers fell from their saddles. Jackson saw what was happening.

"Spread out!" he shouted. "Form a skirmish line."

As ordered, the cavalry troopers dragged carbines from their saddle scabbards, at the same time trying to calm their nervous horses.

"Fire at will!" Jackson shouted. In that instant, his horse was shot out from under him and he managed to avoid being trapped under the animal when it dropped on its side. He grabbed the long gun from the scabbard and took up a position behind the dead animal.

"Get into the rocks, men!" he shouted. "Dismount and take cover!"

Atop the cliff, Jesse James had levered a fresh round into his own rifle. It was he who had shot the Indian decoy, thus alerting the cavalry.

"I think you just started a war, Jesse," his brother commented, as he took aim at an Indian below and on the other side of the canyon. The half-naked man was drawing a bow. Before Frank could trigger a shot, the Indian launched the arrow and dropped out of sight.

"Reckon our kids'll ever b'lieve we was Indian fighters?" Jesse asked. There was a heavy note of irony in his tone. "I'm still looking for Ransom!"

As with most battles, it was difficult to tell who was winning; perhaps, neither side at that point. More cavalry horses were down and several of the troopers had been wounded. Most of Long Arm's men were young and inexperienced with the firearms they carried. All were single-shot rifles left over from the Civil War. Among the arms were 1866 Allin conversion breech-loading rifles that had been adapted from

1863 Springfield muskets. The problem with these rifles was that they all were .50 caliber and ammunition for them was dear. The converted Springfields and their cartridges had been famished by Ransom, who was fully aware they were obsolete.

The cavalry troopers were armed with lever-action repeaters that made up in firepower what they may have lacked in numbers.

Long Arm could see that his warriors were being decimated in spite of the cover they held. Bows and arrows and lances were less than effective at the fifty or more yards to the cavalry troops. He looked around for Jud Ransom, but the rancher had disappeared!

The renegade Indian realized he was losing. It was time to go. He had made the mistake of listening to the grandiose plans of the white-eyed rancher. With Ransom gone, he had to accept the fact that he and his people had been used.

Shouting to his men hidden in the rocks, Long Arm initiated a withdrawal from their positions, Indians individually slipping from cover and moving to where the horses were being held. Long Arm was one of the last to withdraw, telling the others to return to the reservation. He already was lost in the twisting path of the canyon by the time the horse soldiers realized the battle was over and they were able to move into the canyon.

Atop the cliff, Frank and Jesse James withdrew from their position. Clell Miller and Jeb Smith had their sparse camping gear strapped to their horses and stood waiting.

"We goin' now?" Clell wanted to know, unable to hide his anxiety.

Jesse nodded. "We're goin'. Mount up."

"You oughta go down and let them blue bellies know you helped save their bacon," Jeb suggested. Jesse shook his head.

"I think not, Jeb. Let's just find Santa Fe."

Chapter Twenty-Three

With the Navajos apparently gone, Jackson ordered some of his men to set up a defense perimeter, while the other troopers worked at strapping the bodies of dead soldiers across their saddles. Several were badly enough wounded that the troopers had to use lodge poles from nearby groves and blankets to copy the Indian travois that is used to drag the infirmed or often just supplies. In this case, a pole was attached to a stirrup on each side of a cavalry horse, then the blanket lashed between the poles to form a crude cot. There were four dead and seven wounded badly enough that they couldn't sit a horse.

As the measures were being taken, Jackson made notes for his report. Among the rocks, eight Indians had been found dead. It was obvious that the Navajo forces' wounded had been taken with them.

"I don't know what to do with the bodies," the captain muttered, Bard standing at his elbow.

"I reckon they'll come to take them once we're gone," Bard offered. The officer shook his head.

"That's true with the Plains tribes," he acknowledged,

"but the Navajo and Apaches are different. They're fearful of handling dead bodies. Afraid the corpse's spirit will come back to haunt them."

Bard glanced at the sky. Already a dozen or more vultures were circling high overhead. "I guess they'll be taken care of," he offered.

Jackson glanced upward at the top of the cliff on one side of the canyon. "I suspect we owe someone up there a vote of thanks. He hadn't shot that man in the cavalry hat, we'd have ridden right into the trap."

Bard glanced at the top of the escarpment, shaking his head. "I don't reckon you'd find anyone up there to thank, captain."

Jackson cast a glance at him, eyebrow raised. "Oh?"

"I think it was Howard and that bunch of his. I think they're on th' dodge for somethin', but they didn't want to watch us get slaughtered."

Jackson thought about it for a moment, then offered a shrug. "You may be right, but we still don't have Ransom. I want you to take a squad and ride to his ranch. Find him and arrest him!"

Bard nodded, offering a grim smile. "My pleasure, sir. What about Long Arm?"

"We'll assume he's gone back to the reservation. I'll have to deal with the Indian agent on that."

Bard led the contingent of cavalrymen to the ranch on Massacre Mountain, but they knew what they were going to find long before they arrived. The ranch house was ablaze. The corrals were empty of horses.

"No tellin' what went on here," noted the sergeant heading up the cavalry unit. He was looking at the ground. "Plenty of tracks of unshod horses, but they could've been made by horses comin' outa th' corrals."

"Jud Ransom may've come back, cleaned out his safe and fired th' place to help cover his tracks," Bard suggested.

"Reckon we may never know," the sergeant said, turning his horse in the general direction of the fort. "Nobody's had breakfast, Mr. Bard. Maybe we can make th' noon mess!"

Reluctantly, Bard nodded and fell in beside the sergeant as they trotted toward the fort. It wasn't up to him to find the renegade rancher. That was for what they called "higher authority" in military parlance.

It was late afternoon when Captain Jackson sat down at his desk and used pen and paper to outline what he was going to say the next morning, when they buried the troopers slain in the brush with the Navajos. He had done this before after other campaigns, but it never was an easy chore. Whatever one said just didn't seem to be enough.

As for the renegades found dead in the woods facing the main gate, there had been eight of them. He had left it up to Sergeant Major Keene to dispose of their bodies. He pretended not to know what the old soldier's approach would be, but he had seen that before, too, usually with Indians. Keene would find a nearby ravine, dump the bodies into it, then place and explode charges of black powder in the overhang to dump dirt and rock into the natural grave, covering the corpses.

Jogged by his conscience, Jackson had suggested that the sergeant major would offer a few words to send the dead men on their way, but Sergeant Major Keene had no sympathy for anyone involved in killing his horse soldiers.

"They're already in hell, captain. It'd be th' waste of a good prayer," was the old soldier's observation.

"Just do it," the officer ordered. "In this case, you don't have to believe in what you're doing." Disposition of the white renegades' bodies would not be mentioned in his official report.

While the captain pondered, Steve Bard and the contingent of cavalry rode through Fort Wingate's main gate. Without drawing rein, the scout glanced about, surprised at what was happening. Some of the settlers were hitching teams to their wagons. With the crisis ended, it looked as though they were willing to take chances on their own.

Both of the other cavalry troops had returned from their boundary-riding assignment, while Bard and the others had been looking for Ransom. The fort had become a busy place.

Bard stabled his horse, graining the weary animal, then made for his temporary quarters, where he stripped off the leather jacket and donned a light wool shirt that covered the bandage on his chest.

With the buckskin jacket over his arm, he crossed the military street and made for Lane Lester's wagon. She was on her knees beside the wagon, packing a suitcase. Bard halted a few feet away.

"You're leavin'?"

The woman looked up at him, offering a reluctant smile. "There's nothing here for me." Bard extended his arm of which he had draped the buckskin. "I brought back your brother's shirt. Thought you might want to keep it."

Lane rose and glanced at the shirt before she looked into Bard's stoic face. She shook her head. "It seems to fit you, Steve."

"Mighty fine coat. Well made, but I lost some of th' fringe off it."

"You should keep it. One of the ladies here can sew on more fringe." She extended her hand as though to shake the scout's hand, but he simply stared at her. After a moment, Lane dropped her hand, returning his stare as a frown formed on her features.

"It's been nice to know you, Mr. Bard, and I thank you for

what you did to rescue me from Gentleman. You've kept life interesting." She hesitated. "Would you want to help me catch up my team and get them harnessed?"

Bard nodded, suddenly smiling. "I could do that. I think a better idea's for you to kiss me again for luck!"

Lane Lester stared at him for a moment as he allowed the leather jacket to slide off the arm he wrapped around her, pulling her close. The matching of lips seemed experimental for a moment before they got it right.

"Sergeant of the guard! Sergeant of the guard! Post Number One!"

The sentry's anxious cry came from the main gate. Reluctantly, Bard and Lane separated, both staring toward the gate.

"Now what?" Bard muttered. There was a note of disgust in his voice at the interruption. That was enough to cause Lane to giggle.

"I don't think cavalry life really agrees with you," she chided. "Too much interference with our lifestyle!" Both were looking toward the main gate.

Chapter Twenty-Four

The sergeant of the guard was half running toward the main gate, while a few yards behind him lumbered Sergeant Major Keene.

"What is it?" the sharp-featured sergeant demanded as he reached the gate. The sentry motioned toward a small peephole that allowed him to see who was approaching.

"An Injun!" the sentry stated. Even in the uniform, he appeared to be no more than seventeen and probably had lied about his age to enlist.

"One Indian?" the sergeant's tone carried a note of chastisement. "Only one!"

"I think it's that Long Arm." the sentry announced.

Sergeant Major Keene edged past the pair to peer through the peephole. A moment later, he stepped back and nodded at the sentry. "Open the gate!"

The sentry cast him a look of doubt and Keene repeated the order, his tone a bit more harsh.

The gate was swung open and from where Bard and Lane were standing, they could see the single Indian walking his horse toward the fort. Bard recognized the horse as the one once ridden by Jack Gentleman. Long Arm's only armament was a lance, which he carried with the point aimed at the ground. From the other end waved a white rag that called for a truce. Balanced before him on the folded blanket that served in place of a saddle was a bundle wrapped in blood-stained cloth.

"Looks like he's got somethin' in an old flour sack," Bard ventured. The Indian agents had long issued flour as a part of the Navajos' monthly rations. In the beginning, the recipients had not known what to do with it and had smeared it on their faces as what amounted to a cosmetic.

No one spoke as Long Arm slowly rode to within twenty yards of the gate. At that point, he drew his big horse to a halt. He raised his arm and drove the point of the lance into the ground. He stared at the trio standing at the open gate for a moment—Keene, the sentry and the sergeant—then he gripped the top of the blood-stained sack and lowered it to the ground beside the tip of the lance. Without a word, he turned his horse and urged the animal to a gallop.

"What's that all about, sergeant major?" the sergeant wanted to know. "Some kinda Injun hocus-pocus?"

Sergeant Major Keene did not reply. Instead, he turned to the sentry. "Go get it, private. Hand me your rifle."

The sentry hesitated for an instant, staring at the sergeant major to be certain he had heard right. Keene nodded his head in encouragement. "Now!"

The sentry handed the old soldier his rifle and reluctantly marched through the gate. He grabbed the top of the cloth sack, starting to lift it off the ground.

"What's in it?" Keene called. It was obvious he already knew. He'd been fighting Indians for too many years.

The young man opened the sack to look in, then suddenly dropped it. "My, God!" He managed to strangle the words out before he turned his back to the gate to vomit up the day's rations.

Sergeant Major Keene stalked purposefully out to where the sack lay. He reached down to grab it by the bottom, allowing the contents to spill out of the top opening. The bloody head of Jud Ransom rolled in the dust of the entry trail.

Keene turned to look after the rider, but Long Arm had disappeared, hidden in the ravine that had been occupied earlier by the James brothers.

"Reckon we don't hafta look for him no more," the old sergeant major muttered, dropping the sack over the decapitated head. "Shoulda known it don't do to cross an Indian!"